KISS ME GOODNIGHT, SERGEANT MAJOR

The songs and ballads which servicemen made up and sang during World War II have never been published until now; perhaps they were considered too vulgar, too cynical for the delicate sensibilities of those who were not there. One searches for them in vain in official war histories and military memoirs.

This book makes those songs publicly available for the first time – and preserves them before they are forgotten and lost forever. When Martin Page appealed through letters in local newspapers in Britain and the Commonwealth for veterans of the war to write down the songs they remembered, the response was overwhelming. Literally thousands of contributions came in, from which the best and most interesting have been selected.

With sardonic humour, they tell of the Sergeant Major 'who never fired a gun/He won the DCM for things he never done'; of the Yanks who stole their girlfriends back home while they were fighting; of the Twats in the Ops Room; of life in prison camps; of the streets in Cairo 'full of sin and shame'. There are songs of homesickness, of the injustices of officers, of the terrible boredom and occasional heroism of war.

Martin Page has given the full background to each of the songs and – though they may not be great literature – they provide an unusual, fascinating and nostalgic record of life in World War II by the men who fought it.

Being just seven years old on VE Day, Martin Page's participation in World War II was restricted to searching for Nazi spies in the back gardens of Whetstone, London N20, where he lived. As an adult, he has seen service as a correspondent for the *Daily Express* and later for the Thomson Organisation in Algeria, the Congo, the Indo-Pakistan border and Vietnam. His most recent book is *The Company Savage*.

Also by Martin Page

The Company Savage

Kiss Me Goodnight, Sergeant Major

The Songs and Ballads of World War II

Edited by Martin Page

Illustrated by Bill Tidy
Introduction by Spike Milligan

Hart-Davis, MacGibbon   London

Granada Publishing Limited
First published in Great Britain 1973 by Hart-Davis, MacGibbon Ltd
Frogmore, St Albans, Hertfordshire AL2 2NF and
3 Upper James Street, London W1R 4BP

ISBN 0 246 10748 0

Filmset in Photon Imprint 11 on 13 pt. by
Richard Clay (The Chaucer Press), Ltd, Bungay, Suffolk
and printed in Great Britain by
Fletcher & Son Ltd, Norwich

The jacket illustration is from a postcard by Donald McGill,
from the collection of Arthur Calder-Marshall.

Cover design by Ken Carroll

Editor's Note

Many of the authors of these songs have
freely contributed them to this book.
Others are in the public domain. But in
still other cases, the authors are unknown.

In these circumstances, I have instructed
my literary agents to remit a substantial
proportion of any royalty payments they
may receive on my behalf from sales of
this book, directly to organisations
devoted to helping war widows and needy
ex-servicemen of World War II.

To the unknown versifier

Contents

Introduction

by 954024 Gunner Milligan, Spike

'An Army marches on its stomach', said Napoleon. That is so, but its *esprit de corps* is nourished by its songs. Soldiers marching somewhere do it better with marching songs – from Thermopylae to El Alamein, the voices of soldiers singing along dusty roads has been little changed; the ghosts of these marching songs take a long time to lay. I remember my grandmother knowing the words of *Lily Bolero*; it had been a marching song of the Wild Geese!

From the Boer War times I knew *Goodbye, Dolly, I Must Leave You, The Boers Have Taken My Daddy*. When I was but seven, I learnt from my father the marching songs of World War I. *Long Way To Tipperary, Mademoiselle From Armentières, Pack Up Your Troubles*, are still fresh in my mind. In the last war again we marched to new tunes – *You Are My Sunshine, Ma, I Miss Your Apple Pie, Kiss Me Goodnight, Sergeant Major* – and possibly the 'hit' of the war, from the Afrika Korps, *Lili Marlene*. So much for Marching Songs.

Then there was the nostalgic yearning for home songs – sung in pubs or rolling back to billets drunk. It was in these songs the soldier laid bare his otherwise covered-up emotions which poured out after a good night's drinking. They were usually about Mother, the Wife, or the Sweetheart – and in these tear-jerking vocals the singer was soon joined by the rest of the drunks all hanging on to each other – and carrying on despite repeated cries of 'Last orders please, gentlemen'.

The third and last group of songs vary from the light-hearted and bawdy to the obscene. These were usually sung out of earshot of the fair sex, and were often greeted with howls of laughter and earnest cries of 'Encore', and even though I spent seven years in the Army, one kept on hearing new versions. All this compôte of music made life in hard times much easier; music is as much part of war as ammunition.

This Army Song Book should interest not only 'old sweats' but also the public in general.

Spike Milligan

Tracking Down the War Songs

There has been almost a conspiracy of silence over the songs and verses that the people who fought and won World War II made up and sang about it. Most have never been published before; and few people who were not in the forces have even known of their existence.

The explanation for this is, in my opinion, not so much that the songs are liberally sprinkled with four-letter words. Everyone has long been aware that these are as basic to military life as bully beef, and almost nobody could truthfully claim to be shocked by it. Why many of the songs do make disturbing reading for civilians is because of the intensity of the bitterness that comes through the humour – directed, above all, towards the folks back home. This, I think, is why they have been regarded as unsuitable for public consumption.

A couple of summers back, while on a journalistic assignment in the Middle East, I flew into Cairo with my colleague, Ronnie Payne of the *Sunday Telegraph*. Ronnie had previously been in Egypt with the Royal Marines and then as a war correspondent, so it was for him partly a nostalgic return. And as we were driven from the airport to the city, through the chaotic Cairene rush-hour, in a huge and elderly American station-wagon belonging to the Arab League, he suddenly burst into song.

> *They call me Venal Vera, I'm a lovely*
> *from Gezira.*
> *The Führer pays me well for what I do.*
> *The order of the battle, I obtained from*
> *last night's rattle*

> *On the golf course with a brigadier from*
> *'Q' . . .*

He had worked his way through a good half-dozen of the old 8th Army songs by the time we reached the front door of the new Shepheard's Hotel (the old one having been burnt down by rioters in 1956, as a symbol of British military arrogance).

In the bar late that evening, we were joined by two other veterans who also happened to be in Cairo, and the singing session inevitably resumed. It was while they were giving an audience of bemused Egyptians who had quietly gathered a rendering of *Kiss Me Goodnight, Sergeant Major* (their version of which is to be found on page 26), that I was struck by the thought that eventually led to this book.

It was that it would be a sad loss indeed if we allowed these songs to perish by default, by failing to set them down on paper as a permanent record, before they were forgotten for ever. Seized with enthusiasm and a certain amount of whisky, I wrote down those I had heard before I went to bed. Next morning, when I looked at them again, the idea seemed even more important than it had done the night before.

Back in London a few weeks later, I began to make inquiries as to where the songs might be found. The Ministry of Defence, understandably preoccupied with more immediate matters, was not interested.

I approached the Imperial War Museum which, not long before, a pacifist had tried to burn down because he had mistakenly believed it to be devoted to the glorification of war. Mr Lewis, the librarian there and an 8th Army veteran, himself recalled a couple of songs; but the library yielded nothing. Nor did a search through some fifty yards of shelves of books about World War II in the London Library.

Clearly, what had to be done was to launch an appeal to people who had been in the war to come forward with whatever contributions they could offer. One Sunday, I sat at my typewriter and wrote to *The Soldier*, the *Royal British Legion Journal*, the *Ajex Journal*, the TAVR's magazine, the *Corps of Commissionaires*, and about fifty evening and weekly newspapers around Britain.

I wrote: 'Before they are all forgotten for ever, I am trying to collect as many as possible of the songs servicemen made up and sang in World War II . . . I should like to appeal to all people who served in the war to search their memories, write down any songs that come back to them and send them to me.'

The response was astonishing. People rushed up to their attics, hunted through piles of dusty old papers and found words to songs they had noted down over a quarter of a century ago, and almost forgotten about until they read my letter.

Others racked their brains and wrote down what they could recall. That so many could remember so much after all this time was in itself a remarkable commendation of the songs and their mostly unknown authors.

Quite a few were unable to send songs, but did put me in touch with various people who could. And a surprising

number simply wrote to encourage me, and to urge me to publish a book of them.

In less than a month, I received over three hundred replies from every major town and city, and many minor ones, in Britain.

James Pettigrew, who had flown for the Navy in the war and was editing the *Sunday Mirror*'s gossip column, wrote an article about my quest. A result of that was an invitation to appear on BBC Radio's 'Today' programme. With Malcolm Billington, the interviewer, I duly went before the microphone and we read aloud together selections from the contributions I had received.

This produced another flood of mail. Some protested that their favourites had been left out, and sent them in. P. A. McKenzie of Bolton summed up the reaction of a lot of listeners: 'Having switched on your "Today" programme at about 7.00 a.m. this morning and then as usual ignored it, I suddenly found myself hearing that dreadful verse starting, "The colonel kicks the major . . ." And having perpetrated it myself in the ablutions of 11th King's C Company at about 6.30 a.m., September 1940, I suddenly found myself taken from the unpleasant security of 1972 into the exciting opposite . . .'

I then wrote to an Australian friend, John Tidey of the *Melbourne Age*, whom I had first met when we were reporting the Nigerian–Biafran war together, and asked him to find out what ex-ANZACs had to offer.

As I had done in Britain, John wrote to newspapers around the country. Once again, the response was astonishing. He received about two hundred replies.

Over the next year, I myself followed

up leads I had been given, made contacts in other countries and received more and more contributions.

It is interesting that nobody anywhere submitted *Keep the home fires burning*, or *There'll always be an England* (although we did get *There'll always be an England – while Australia be there*) or *We'll hang out our washing on the Siegfried Line*, which civilians fondly imagined to be the forces' favourites.

Some lady members of the home front, whom I have dubbed (I hope not unkindly) the Patriotic Poetesses, sent in their wartime compositions like:

> *Who said decadent England?*
> *Who said lazy and soft? . . .*

and the *Bootle Air-Raid Shelter Song*, that jauntily declares:

> *And when the battle has been won,*
> *We'll think of those that have passed on.*

But the contributions from those who had served in the war were of a different tone. They told of a sergeant major:

> *. . . He never fired a gun.*
> *He won the DCM for things he never done.*

Of McKafferty who, incensed at being ordered to take the names of some soldiers' children playing harmlessly in the barrack square, ends up shooting the colonel, and being hanged himself.

They told of the earwigs on the floors 'who curl up and then form fours'; of 'stew for breakfast, stew for tea'; of a 'flea-bound, bug-bound dug-out in Matru'; of the 'wrennery' being put out of bounds; of 'Christmas Day in the Brown House':

> *And the Nazis were seated there,*
> *Bawling their party war-cries*
> *And swilling their ersatz beer.*

There was the transport sergeant in the desert who, while having some lunch said:

> *Now boys, I've got a hunch.*
> *Why don't we grease all our nipples today,*
> *So we can run faster when we run away.*

There was the red-light street in Cairo 'full of sin and shame', and the old Australian cottage:

> *With roses round the door,*
> *Where a girl received a letter,*
> *A letter from the war.*
> *With her mother's arms around her,*
> *She gave way to sobs and sighs . . .*

And the soldier being cuckolded while he's away fighting (many were):

> *See him waiting every morning, for the highly-treasured mail,*
> *Knowing what he'll find in it – once again the same old tale.*
> *Oh, how often have I seen it, watched the agonising face . . .*

I believe that these songs, more than anything else to have come out of the war, portray what it was actually like to be in it. With the notable exception of Mr Spike Milligan's memoirs of his life as a private soldier, *Adolf Hitler – My Part In His Downfall*, most books about it have been written by officers and military historians. The latter tend to have a weakness for studying battles by building table-top models of the terrain over which they were fought, and deploying their regiments of toy soldiers. They call this 'playing war-games', and their accounts of World War II are in character.

Television and films offer a glamorised view of what the war was like. They present the men as steely, fearless (that is, numbskulled) patriots, ever ready to do and die for the sake of Old England.

The fact is that most of the men in the war on our side hated almost every moment of it, and for much of the time were thoroughly scared. Nobody in their senses wants to be the man whose life is sacrificed for the cause.

Why have we gone along with such a false and sentimental picture of them? Perhaps because we should prefer not to contemplate the fact that many of those who bravely risked and lost their lives begrudged having to do so, to say the least, and were far from convinced that the rest of us, on whose behalf they did so, were worth it.

Alan Morehead, the great *Daily Express* war correspondent, wrote in his diaries after the crucial battle of Longstop Hill in Tunisia in 1943, about visiting some troops in the trenches:

> There were several old papers lying about. One, the *Daily Mirror*, had its last page turned upward and its thick headline read: 'No more wars after this, says Eden.'
>
> Seeing me look at it, the soldier on the end of the trench said bitterly: 'They said the last war was going to end all wars. I reckon this war is supposed to start them all again.'
>
> When they read the war correspondents' badges on our shoulders . . . they asked: 'Are you the bastard that wrote in the paper that we were getting poached egg for breakfast every morning?' . . . They were hostile, bitter and contemptuous.
>
> They hated the war . . . They fought because they were part of a system, part of a team. It was something they were obliged to do, and now that they were in it they had a technical interest and pride in it. They wanted to win and get out of it – the sooner the better. They had no high notions of glory.
>
> A great number of people at home who referred emotionally to 'Our Boys' would have been shocked and horrified if they had known just how the boys were thinking and behaving. They would have regarded them as young hooligans. And this was because the real degrading nature of war was not understood by the public at home, and it can never be understood by anyone who has not spent months in the trenches or in the air or at sea.

In compiling this book, it was brought home to me that this is a bitterness that still lingers on in the minds of some of the men who were there. One letter, enclosing four songs, from a holder of the Military Medal, said: 'I served in several theatres of war – France, Western Desert (I am an ex-Desert Rat), Italy and Germany. After my army service, I got married and now lead a pretty staid life with my wife and three children, and often wondered whether it was worth it.

'I live in a slum and am ashamed of it but cannot do anything about it, as I am just a poor disabled working man. Perhaps you can understand how bitter I feel, to think that after I and thousands of other men fought for this country, we come back here to live like this.'

This book basically consists of servicemen's songs about the war, and not – with one exception – officially-approved ones. I have tried to rigorously exclude the commercial products of Tin Pan Alley, whose operators were as quick to catch on to popular trends during the war, as they are today. Almost none that I have included were written by professionals, and I have not allowed literary criteria to guide me in my selection. By the same token, I have resisted temptations to 'improve' them by correcting their scansion, etc., and have presented them as far as possible as they were received and, presumably, as they were actually sung.

The great majority are based on familiar tunes – hymns, folk songs, music-hall songs and the like. Where possible, I have given the name of the tune with each song.

A problem I have repeatedly encountered is that similar songs have a tendency to crop up in different situations. Many readers will, I am sure, feel that I have got some of the songs 'wrong', or attributed one or another of 'their's' to another unit. I am sorry about this, but there is nothing that can be done about it. To publish every variation of every song would result in a repetitive and tedious book. To know by whom and where and when each song was first sung, is impossible. Over some of them, rival claims are lodged by men who served in places as distant as Halkirk in Scotland and Tobruk, and in units as different as the British paratroopers and the Australian infantry. It is not for me to act as referee, and I have no intention of getting caught in the cross-fire.

I recognise that despite the kindness and the co-operation of over five hundred people who have helped me, this collection is not, and could not be, definitive. I invite any readers with protests, corrections, suggestions or additions to write to me, care of the publishers.

Meanwhile, I should like to acknowledge humbly and gratefully the help so many have given me. I regret that there is insufficient space to thank them all by name in these pages – over twenty people sent me *The D-Day Dodgers* alone – and I hope that they will understand that their contributions have been highly valued.

MARTIN PAGE

1

I
Don't Want to
Go to War

I DON'T WANT TO BE A SOLDIER
'I'd sooner . . . live on the earnings of a high born lady.'

Belisha's Army

The British and other governments of the Empire, having declared war on 3 September 1939, had to hurriedly recruit men to fight it. Within weeks, the new conscripts in training camps all over Britain were to be heard singing this song. (Leslie Hore-Belisha was then the Secretary of State for War.)

We had to join. We had to join.
We had to join Belisha's Army.
Fourteen bob a week,
Fuck-all to eat,
Marching round the square
With bloody great blisters on our feet.

We had to join. We had to join.
We had to join Belisha's Army.
If it wasn't for the war,
We'd have fucked off long before.
Hore-Belisha – You're barmy.

Waltzing Into Flinders

Australians loyally rose to answer the call of the Motherland in her hour of need. Many signed up with the Navy and were sent to Flinders, the naval base in Victoria.

We went to join the navy,
Walking up on air,
Waltzing into Flinders,
Thought we were nearly there.

CHORUS
But now that the time has come to pass
You can stick the navy up your arse.
We signed away our freedom
We signed away our souls.

We never heard of jaunties,
Never heard of rounds,
Never knew the wrennery
Was out of bloody bounds.

CHORUS

I Don't Want To Be A Soldier

After delays caused by disorganisation and shortage of ships, the first units of the British Expeditionary Force landed in France at the end of September. As they rode in the backs of lorries towards the German lines, they sang:

I don't want to be a soldier,
I don't want to go to war.
I'd sooner hang around
Piccadilly underground,
Living on the earnings of a high-born lady.

Don't want a bullet up me arsehole,
Don't want me bollocks shot away.
I'd rather live in England,
In merry, merry England,
And fornicate me fucking life away.

No More Soldiering For Me

To Hitler's increasing fury, the German High Command delayed launching an attack on the West through the autumn. The winter came and caused further delays. And then a staff officer lost his way and arrived in the West with a complete set of German invasion plans, which had to be radically revised as a result.

During the 'phoney war' the troops stuck in France borrowed a refrain from World War I.

To the tune of 'What A Friend We Have in Jesus'

When this bleeding war is over,
Oh how happy I shall be.
When I get my civvy clothes on,
No more soldiering for me.
No more church parades on Sundays,
No more calling of the roll,
No more blancoing equipment,
NO SALUTING FOR THE DOLE!

An alternative ending was:

No more asking for a pass.
We can tell the Sergeant Major
TO STICK HIS PASSES UP HIS ARSE.

You Take The Gun

On 10 May 1940 – the day Winston Churchill became Prime Minister – the Germans attacked and broke through the Western defences. The British went into action for the first time.

To the tune of 'Loch Lomond'

Oh, I'll take the tripod,
And you take the gun,
And you'll be in action before me.
And if you get shot,
Then I'll take the blooming lot,
And I'll eat your iron rations in the morning.

The Old Diehards

Some of the troops being held in reserve back in Britain sang:

Oh please don't send away the old diehards,
Oh please don't send away the boys.
Every man in the regiment is willing
To do or die – we don't think.
Oh please don't send away the old diehards,
They're second to the navy on the sea.
If it wasn't for the old diehards,
Where would England be?
Blowed if we know.
Where would England be?

The Manchester Lads

In the face of the threat of imminent German invasion, the National Defence Corps – soon renamed the Home Guard – was formed of volunteers unfit for one reason or another for full-time military service.

To be declaimed in a Mancunian accent

Shall I tell you how I joined up sir?
I will if you listen to me.
At Manchester Free-Trade Hall
I answered the call
And became an NDC.

Our officer wasn't so bad sir,
He just messed and mucked us about,
We got knocked knees
With forming threes,
And he turned us inside out.

He took us on long marches,
That made us all feel queer,
We was all dead beat,
Had corns on our feet,
Could hardly walk to the hut for beer.

Our officer was a good sort,
I even like to mention,
He even gave us time off,
To draw our old age pension.

The kids they all followed us,
Dogs and all
Gazing at us old sweats
Who answered England's call.

So cheer up my lads,
Have this drink on me,
England will never be in danger,
Not while there's an NDC.

From A Dying Soldier To His Love

In France, the British were being sent tumbling back towards the Channel coast.
Casualties were heavy.

> My lonely little sweetheart in the spring,
> Those wedding bells for you will never ring.
> Your lover is a-lying
> On the battlefield a-dying,
> My lonely little sweetheart in the spring.

Down By St Valery

After only a fortnight's fighting, the British forces were in a hopeless situation, and the decision was taken to withdraw.

Most of the troops made it to the Dunkirk beaches. But others, including the 51st Highland Division, had been cut off. They fought their way to the small fishing village of St Valery-en-Caux, far to the south, where a memorial now stands to them.

> The Highland Division, they fought and they fell,
> Although they were battered by shot and by shell,
> Yet they were determined to fight and go free,
> Down by St Valery.
>
> That night on the cliff tops, I'll never forget,
> As we lay on the ground and it was soaking wet.
> These memories will ever last for aye,
> Down by St Valery.
>
> The planes high above us kept dropping their bombs,
> When we on the ground kept on singing our songs.
> They thought they had got us, but they were wrong,
> Down by St Valery.

Then far out at sea, we spied the Boys in Blue,
Came for to carry us home.
There's a debt that we owe them we can never repay,
There's a debt we will owe them for many a day,
And each night in our prayers we will always say,
God Bless the Boys in Blue.

In A German Prison

Some, although they survived, never made it to the ships at all, and did not see Britain again for five years.

This song was overheard by a prisoner in a German POW camp – he never knew who sang it. It is based on an older, civilian prison song.

It was in a German prison
That a British soldier lay.
He was writing to his mother,
Who was many miles away.

He wrote, 'Dear mother darling,
I do hope you will understand.
I was fighting for Old England,
When I fell in German hands.

'But when this war is over,
And the victory is won,
I will come back to you, dear mother,
And remain, your loving son.'

2

We Had a Sergeant Major

KISS ME GOODNIGHT, SERGEANT MAJOR
'Kiss me goodnight, Sergeant Major.
Tuck me in my little wooden bed.'

Kiss Me Goodnight, Sergeant Major

At lights-out time in the barracks, as the Sergeant Major made the last round of his charges, the latter would raucously serenade him with this old English song. It somehow never seemed the same from the lips of Vera Lynn.

Kiss me goodnight, Sergeant Major.
Tuck me in my little wooden bed.
We all love you, Sergeant Major,
When we hear you calling – 'Show a leg!'
Don't forget to wake me in the morning
And bring me up a nice hot cup of tea.
Kiss me goodnight, Sergeant Major.
Sergeant Major, be a mother to me.

Our Sergeant

We had a Sergeant Major, who never fired a gun,
He won the DCM for things he never done.
And when the shells came over, you should see the bastard run
Oh! Miles behind the lines.

He'll Be There

Oh, I'll never forget the day that I enlisted on the spree,
To be a greasy Gunner in the Royal Artillery.
Oh, my heart is aching and 'tis breaking
To be in civvy street once more.
You ought to see the fellows on a Friday night,
Polishing up their buttons in the pale moonlight.

For there's going to be Inspection in the morning,
The Battery Sergeant Major will be there.
He'll be there, he'll be there,
In that little wooden hut across the square.
When we're crying out for water,
He'll be hugging the colonel's daughter,
In that little wooden hut across the square.

Our Windy Sergeant

He's a windy sergeant, oh! What a windy sergeant,
Early in the morning when his boys are standing-to,
He's fucking round the barracks with his four-by-two.

He's a windy sergeant, windy as the flowers in May,
Fighting for his King and Country,
Sitting on his arse all day.

Sod 'Em All

To the tune of 'Bless 'Em All'

Sod 'em all. Sod 'em all,
The long and the short and the tall,
Sod all the sergeants and WO ones,
Sod all the corporals and their bastard sons,
For we're saying goodbye to them all,
As back to their billets they crawl,
You'll get no promotion
This side of the ocean,
So cheer up, my lads, sod 'em all.

THE SARN'T MAJOR'S BALLS
'The crowds they do muster to gaze at the cluster.'

The Sarn't Major's Balls

To the tune of 'The Bells of St Mary's'

The balls of Sarn't Major are wrinkled and crinkled,
Capacious and spacious as the dome of St Paul's.
The crowds they do muster to gaze at the cluster,
They stop and they stare at that glorious pair
Of Sarn't Major's Balls.
Balls, Balls, Balls, Balls, Balls, Balls, Balls, Balls!

(the last line on a descending scale, like a chime)

The Pansy Pleat

The NCOs had something to say back, of course. This is a prime example, written by a lance-corporal, that shows the Australian's traditional dislike of 'effeminacy'.

Before he joined the Army
And settled down in camp,
He used to be a city lair
Whom certain girls would vamp.

The coat he wore was 'Calendar'
So short it showed the date.
He donned a perky 'pork-pie' hat
The envy of his mate.

And now he's in the Army
He tries to be the same,
With 'pansy pleat' in soldier's hat
And 'lair' is still his name.

His marcel waves peep out beneath
A wrongly worn chapeau.
He leaves his tunic neck agape
His swan-like throat to show.

He thinks it makes him look the part,
A soldier every inch.
But say old chap that's where you're wrong,
Just give yourself a pinch.

And you will wake and realise
That there is something fine
In wearing such a uniform
'My friend' as yours and mine.

It symbolises something
That words cannot explain,
That was a war some years ago
And 'Dig', it will again.

So don't adopt the 'pansy pleat'
And try to be a 'lair',
But wear it like a man
And shout 'Australia will be there'.

Lance-Corporal B. R. Grosvenor

3

The Nazi Gang

HITLER HAS ONLY GOT ONE BALL
'Hitler has only got one ball.'

Hitler Has Only Got One Ball

Perhaps the most popular song of the war both among troops and on the home front, *Hitler Has Only Got One Ball* unexpectedly became the subject of an intense, scholarly and lengthy debate, conducted largely through the columns of the *New Statesman*, in the spring of 1973.

It was begun by Michael Graubert, who wrote to the editor pointing out that the Soviet autopsy on Hitler's body, details of which were not published until many years after the war, reportedly found that the late Nazi leader had possessed, in fact, but one testicle. The pertinent question he raised was whether or how the author of the song, which was in wide circulation as early as 1940, had known.

This was a problem that had been preoccupying me for some time, and I passed to the *New Statesman* one of the speculations I had come across. It was that Unity Mitford, whose close friendship with Hitler before the war had occasioned adverse comment in Britain, had actually been motivated by selfless patriotism, and had been a British spy. (This would, of course, put her suicide by shooting in the Englischer Garten in Munich – which some of her London acquaintances had regarded as another instance of her penchant for exhibitionist melodrama – in an entirely new light, indeed cast doubts on whether it was suicide at all.)

According to the speculation, Miss Mitford, having discovered her 'friend's' mono-testicularity, smuggled the intelligence back to His Majesty's Government. It eventually found its way to a top-secret psychological warfare team operating in Oxford Street, composed of psychoanalysts and professional musicians who worked together on a brief to drive Hitler ever madder by devising well-aimed insults against him and setting them to music.

Could it have been they who produced *Hitler Has Only Got One Ball*? Perhaps it was insidiously promoted by means of the plain-clothes psy-war agents who, as everybody knew, were to be found in pubs all over the country, propping up the bars and the customers' morale?

Many far more eccentric projects of this kind had indeed been carried out during the war; but the theory found little favour with other participants in the debate. Most appeared to consider the accusation of mono-testicularity to be too obvious to warrant specific explanation in this case.

William Manley wrote that 'It occurs to me to suggest, with all due humility, that

Hitler
Has only got one ball

appeared merely because of the spirit of the times and the fact that the words happened to fit. In earlier times and different circumstances, it might have been

Cardinal Wolsey
Has only got one vinegar-soaked orange

or

Francis Lord Veralum
Has only got one terrestial globe

(though the note values might have to be changed a bit). Is it really necessary to assume prior knowledge on the part of the poet? Shakespeare made a clock chime in

Julius Caesar; does this mean that he knew some bright Roman was a bit ahead of his time?'

From Oxford, Christine S. Nicolls opined, a little loftily: 'We British have a conspicuous capacity for anglicising the pronunciation of foreign names that do not slip easily off our tongues. We find it more comfortable to pronounce Goebbels as "Goballs". The step from here to "Noballs" is irresistible, at least to any lewd versifier.

'May I suggest, therefore, that it was this obvious rhyme which prompted the verse denigrating the virility of the leaders of our former enemies, rather than any deficiency in Hitler's private parts? After all, the criticisms that can be made of people's genitalia are limited in scope, and clearly somebody had to be the possessor of but one testicle. In this verse, that fate fell to Hitler.'

Michael Flanders, the well-known lyricist and comedian, entered the fray with a brilliant and learned contribution. 'Reference to the author of *Hitler Has Only Got One Ball* – I believe it was some young man from Devizes – brings to mind the great original songs of earlier wars. Of Kaiser Bill ("he's only got one pill") and His Little Willie; and from the Transvaal, the ballad of Kruger ("Oom Paul, he's only got one ball") and General Smuts ("he's lost one of his nuts").

'One compares Dibdin's patriotic *Singular Case of an Upstart Frog* (1797):

. . . Alas poor Frenchie Buonaparte Hath but one, on its own, apart!

CHORUS
Hussa for the seamen of England, Jack Tar will strain his rowlocks, etc.

Loss of one testicle is, of course, no bar to paternity, a popular misconception enshrined in another old and often bowdlerised song, *You can't have bred with but one ball*. What a colourful TV series it would all make – and here at last is a theme from which women are excluded. Though I suppose something might be done with Madame Bovary.'

The debate ground to a splendidly *New Statesman*-ish halt with a contribution from a Mr Peter Sharples of Marylebone High Street, London W1, which appeared to accuse those of us who had participated in it of being guilty of indifference towards conditions prevailing in Pentonville Prison.

In the meantime, an informant who wished to remain anonymous had given me information which seemed to resolve this great historical mystery.

'Some time in 1938,' she wrote, 'I spent a few days on the South Coast with the five-year-old son of friends who was recovering from a slight illness; and as it was a sunny day, I let him run around on the beach.

'Presently, I saw him playing with two children whom he dragged along to me, saying he could not understand what they were saying. I am Danish and bilingual in German – neither was of any use. Then a tall woman appeared, their Nurse, and she and I fell into conversation as she knew German.

'She was in fact Czech and told me that she had escaped overnight with the children and their parents from Prague, as the children's father – a bank director – had received warnings of the imminent arrival of the Germans.

'As for Hitler – he was "quite mad", and she had known for years that he had been wounded in the first world war, since when "*ihm felt einer*" – he lacks one.

'I was young at the time, and green as a lettuce-leaf, but as she lowered her voice when she told me this, I guessed that it might be embarrassing to enquire further. I have since grasped the meaning of her remark.'

Disappointingly mundane though this clue was, it had a ring of authenticity. Subsequent inquiries established that the rumour had indeed been widespread in Central Europe in the late 1930s. On the other hand, there was also a popular ballad in the USA in the nineteenth century about a trade union leader, which began:

> *Arthur Hall*
> *Has only got one ball*

Meanwhile, *Hitler Has Only Got One Ball* seems to have followed the fate of so many other lewd and political songs of the past, and to have become – in a highly corrupted version – a kind of alternative or underground nursery rhyme which can be heard in playgrounds all over Britain. The version runs:

> *Hitler has only got one ball,*
> *The other is in the old town hall.*
> *His mother, she pinched the other,*
> *Now Hitler ain't got none at all.*

To the tune of 'Colonel Bogey'

Hitler
Has only got one ball!
Goering
Has two, but very small!
Himmler
Has something similar,
But poor old Goebbels
Has no balls
At all!

Christmas Day In The Brown House

It was Christmas Day in the Brown House,
And the Nazis were seated there,
Bawling their party war-cries,
And swilling their ersatz beer.

Then up spake their mighty Führer,
He was smiling a sickly smile,
'I wish you a happy Christmas.'
And the Nazis answered, 'Heil.'

'I have given you guns for butter,
I have given you 'planes and tanks,
I have given you my New Order.'
And the Nazis murmured, 'Thanks.'

'What would you like for Christmas?
Well, now we must face the facts.
I haven't much more to give you,
Except for some broken pacts.'

'You won't have a Christmas pudding,
For the cupboard is almost bare;
But I call on you all to STICK IT.'
And the Nazis queried, 'Where?'

My Cousins

I've got cousins all over the place –
England, Ireland, Scotland and Wales,
Russia, Prussia and Jerusalem.
I don't care if he's the leader
Of the Deutschland Friede,
Fuck him – he's no cousin of mine.

The Nazi Gang

We came to fight in Egypt,
Just to fight the Nazi gang.
When we catch their big-shots,
Sure we'll see them hang.
We'll make a start with Hitler,
And he the price will pay,
For all his dirty murders.
And then we can all say:
He bombed our homes,
Filled them with mud,
And down our street there flowed the blood.
The AFS played their part well –
They put out fires as hot as hell.
Our women folk hung on with all their might
Till Germany had lost its fight.
And when this war is over,
Back to civvy street we'll go,
To take the baby's bottle,
And the garden seeds to sow.
We'll put our working clothes on,
And run to catch the tram.
We'll come home to dinner,
To great plates of eggs and ham.

B. Barnes

4

Military Life

OH! FUCKING HALKIRK
'All fucking clouds, all fucking rain,
No fucking kerbs, no fucking drains.'

Something many civilians fail to understand about war is how little time during one, those who are in the forces actually spend fighting it.

You wait about almost interminably, while officers and NCOs dream up stupid things for you to do to pass the time. You board a train or a ship for a secret destination and when you finally arrive and have gone through the ritual chaos of disembarkation, find yourself hanging around again.

Outside A Lunatic Asylum

Kindly contributed by Spike Milligan.

Outside a lunatic asylum one day,
A gunner was picking up stones.
Up popped a lunatic and said to him:
'Good morning, Gunner Jones,
How much a week do you get for doing that?'
'Fifteen bob,' I cried.
He looked at me
With a look of glee,
And this is what he cried:

'Come inside, you silly bugger, come inside, come inside.
I thought you had a bit more sense,
Working for the army. Take my tip,
Act a bit barmy and become a lunatic.
You get your four meals regular
And two new suits beside.
Wot? Fifteen bob a week,
A wife and kids to keep?
Come inside, you silly bugger, come inside.'

The Colonel Kicks The Major

To the tune of 'Macnamara's Band'

Oh, the colonel kicks the major,
And the major has a go.
He kicks the poor old captain,
Who then kicks the NCO.
And as the kicks get harder,
They are passed on down to me.
And I am kicked to bleeding hell
To save democracy.

Question And Answer

To the tune of 'Little Brown Jug'

From: Cpl. X

I've sent the roses, bought the wine,
Can I go home and claim what's mine?
The debts are piling, there's bills to pay,
The milkman calls five times a day.
The weather's lousy, I'm growing old,
Her bed is warm but mine is cold.
No more in Shropshire I wish to roam,
For God's sake Guv, let me go home.

Reply by Sqn. Comd.

The roses arrived from me she thought,
Ref. your wine, I've drunk the last draught.
The debts I've paid, I'm rich you see.
The milkman calls to spy for me.
You're growing old so you say,
So do I, day by day.
Her bed is warm 'cause I'm there too,
Please understand no room for you.
So in Shropshire you must roam,
It's the Sqn. Ldr. who's going home.

D. L. J.

McCafferty

When I was eighteen years of age,
To join the Army sure I did engage;
And so it happened I was sent
To join the Forty Second Regiment.

Now all young soldiers listen to me,
Just take a word of warning from me;
To Fulward Barracks I did go
To serve my time there in the GB Depot.

One day on duty at the gate
Some soldiers' children were playing late
Across the square the captain came,
And made me take those little children's names.

I took one name instead of three,
Neglect of duty was charged against me,
And so, it was for being kind
Seven days to barracks sure I was confined.

Next day upon the barrack square
With pack and rifle I was there
I SHOT THE COLONEL! 'Twas not meant.
To lame that captain sure was my intent.

To Liverpool assizes I did go,
To stand my trial for this great woe.
The Judge he said, 'McCafferty,
For this you'll die upon the gallows tree.'

I have no father to take my part,
Nor yet a mother to break her heart;
One friend I have, and a woman is she,
Who'd lay down her life just for McCafferty.

Now all young soldiers, take warning from me,
Just do your duty and do it free;
And take away these words from me,
There's another in the ranks just like McCafferty.

Larkhill

To the tune of 'Down Home in Tennessee'

Down home in Larkhill Camp,
That's where you get the cramp,
Through laying in the damp,
In a tent without a lamp.
All I can dream of each night,
Is a field of snowy white,
With sergeants calling,
Lance-jacks bawling,
And I wake up in a fright.

The earwigs on the floors
Curl up and then form fours,
And then there are the ants,
Who dress up in your pants.
And early every morning,
The bugle goes without a warning,
Get out of bed there!
Show a leg there!
And get out on parade!

Longmoor

To the tune of 'The Mountains of Mourne'

Oh Mary, this Longmoor's a wonderful place,
But the system they have here's a fucking disgrace.
There's lots of bands playing, and bugles galore,
And the whole fucking thing is a fucking great bore.

There's plenty of NAAFI tea, oh never mind.
It's a brew I'm sure Brooke Bonds never designed.
The flavour I'm sure no one ever could place,
But really it's a mixture of polish and paste.

This Longmoor on Thursdays is lovely to see,
With Sappers all lined up in columns of three,
'Tis time when the officers sit in their chairs,
And dish out the money as if it was their's.

When you get to them you hand them your book,
Then all you get from them's a dirty black look.
They give you the cash you've fucking well earned,
And before you get out, in the box it's returned.

They tell us on Sundays it's a day we can rest,
But we're out in the morning in best battle dress.
They tell us as Christians to church we must go,
So we're lined up once more in threes in a row.

They tell us that some day this war's going to end,
And a nice load of cash we'll be able to spend.
Then it's goodbye to the army, goodbye to the tea,
And a SOLDIER'S FAREWELL TO THE OLD C.R.E.

Oh! Fucking Halkirk

In 1941, having been scattered across the Orkney and Shetland islands, part of the Ayrshire Yeomanry (The Earl of Carrick's Own) found itself back on the mainland at Halkirk, in Caithness.

To the tune of 'So Early in the Morning' (adapted)

This fucking town's a fucking cuss.
No fucking trams, no fucking bus.
Nobody cares for fucking us,
In fucking Halkirk.

The fucking roads are fucking bad,
The fucking folk are fucking mad,
It makes the brightest fucking sad,
In fucking Halkirk.

All fucking clouds, all fucking rain,
No fucking kerbs, no fucking drains.
The council's got no fucking brains,
In fucking Halkirk.

No fucking sport, no fucking games,
No fucking fun. The fucking dames
Won't even give their fucking names,
In fucking Halkirk.

Everything's so fucking dear –
A fucking bob for fucking beer.
And is it good? No fucking fear,
In fucking Halkirk.

The fucking flicks are fucking old,
The fucking seats are always sold,
You can't get in for fucking gold,
In fucking Halkirk.

The fucking dances make you smile.
The fucking band is fucking vile.
It only cramps your fucking style,
In fucking Halkirk.

Best fucking place is fucking bed,
With fucking ice on your fucking head.
You might as well be fucking dead,
In fucking Halkirk.

No fucking grub, no fucking mail,
Just fucking snow and fucking hail.
In anguish deep, we fucking wail,
In fucking Halkirk.

The fucking pubs are fucking dry.
The fucking barmaid's fucking fly.
With fucking grief we fucking cry
OH! FUCK HALKIRK!

Tatton Parachute Training School

To the tune of 'The Mountains of Mourne'

Oh Mary, this Tatton's a wonderful sight,
With the paratroops jumping by day and by night.
They land on potatoes and barley and corn,
And there's gangs of them wishing they'd never been born.

At least, when I asked them, that's what I was told,
The jumping is easy, slow pairs leave them cold.
They said that they'd rather bale out of the moon,
Than jump any more from that fucking balloon.

The Marching Song Of The Warwickshire Yeomanry

To the tune of 'If Moonshine Don't Kill Me, I'll Live Till I Die'

Oh merry, oh merry,
Oh merry are we.
We are the Warwickshire Yeomanry.
Sing hi, sing lo,
Wherever we go,
The Warwickshire Yeomanry never say no.
We can ride,
We can fight,
We can fuck all the night.
We are the prostitute's pride and delight.

The Marching Song Of The Border Regiment

We are the Minden Dandies, straight from the west,
Some of the latest, and some of the best.
We join in royalty wherever we go.
But where we come from, nobody knows.

They call us the pride of the ladies, the ladies.
They take all our wages, our wages, our wages.
We are respected wherever we roam.
We are the Minden Dandies.

Sick Parade

Ronald F. Palmer, the author of the next three items, and of others elsewhere in the book, was one of the most prolific military versifiers of World War II. Unfortunately, he seems to have completely disappeared since, but seems to have come originally from the north-west of England.

When reveille blew this morning
And my head I slowly raised,
I sank back upon my pillow
Feeling tired out and dazed.
As the sergeant shouted 'Turn Out!'
With a glassy eye I gazed.

For my tummy it was aching,
From a binge the night before.
In my head a thousand devils
Danced and made my poor eyes sore;
So at nine I dragged my body
Through the MO's open door.

Many more were there beside me
In a long unbroken line,
But I felt that no one's illness
Could be quite as bad as mine,
And the MO gave some aspirins,
And to some a 'Number Nine'.

'Sir, my abdomen is aching,'
But the MO answered, 'Nuts!
Officers have abdomens, lad,
That's what the Almighty puts!
Sergeants and above have stomachs,
But you privates just have – GUTS!'

Then he gave me a white powder,
Marked me down for 'M and D',
Told the Company Sergeant Major
Just what was amiss with me,
So tonight instead of drinking,
Doing pack drill I shall be.

Reveille

When out of sleep you're wakened in the middle of the night,
And the sergeant shouts out 'wakey' as he switches on the light,
And you're sure that you're still dreaming and you can't have heard aright,
That's reveille!

When you cower 'neath the blankets on a cold and frosty morn,
Till the sergeant spots you and the blankets from your bed are torn,
And you curse the whole damned army and the day that you were born,
That's reveille!

When you wake with head that's throbbing from the binge the night before
And the bugle blows so loudly right outside the billet door,
And you swear you'll never mix your beer with spirits any more,
That's reveille!

If you are a gay Lothario and you stay out very late
With a lady who adores you and desires to meet her fate,
If you hear a bugle calling as you reach the barrack gate,
That's 'Reveille!'

Red Cap

You look so fierce and terrible,
As with your lead, indelible,
   You write my misdeeds in your little book.
Because my boots are dirty
You get quite annoyed and shirty,
   And make me out to be a bloomin' crook.

When I go on a promenade
With Susan, Joan or Adelaide,
   Your red cap haunts me everywhere I go.
I can't undo a button,
And my suede shoes I daren't put on,
   For if I'm caught, whatever shall I do?

You must delight in whitening
Your lance-stripe; it's so frightening
   To privates of the line as you approach.
We know 'twill be the guard room
When you find us in the card room
   Of an 'Out of Bounds' casino, drinking hooch.

I've dodged your kind from Salisbury Plain
To far Hong Kong and home again,
   And learned to hate your red caps more and more.
In Singapore you chased me,
And in Mandalay you traced me,
   As the man who brought discredit to his corps.

You chased me through the corridors,
With all the skill of toreadors,
   Of every red light house in Sister Street.
And as proof of your attentions
I still bear your names and 'mentions',
   In evidence upon my conduct sheet.

Yet on the Dunkirk beaches, you
Kept calm and knew just what to do,
    And we for you had admiration deep.
But tonight I have a date, sir,
And I'm going to stay out late, sir,
    So please, dear Red Cap, just go home and sleep!

Puckapunyal

Puckapunyal was a military training camp outside Melbourne, still in use today.

To the tune of 'Bye-bye, Blackbird'

Pack up all your bags and kit,
Puckapunyal's up to shit,
Bye-bye, Pucka.
Stew for breakfast,
Stew for tea,
No more bloody stew for me,
Bye-bye, Pucka.

No more hiking over bloody mountains,
We'll be drinking Fosters out of fountains.

No more blanco,
No more brass,
You can stick 'em up your arse.
Pucka, bye-bye!

'HOUSEY-HOUSEY'
*'A single line wins thirty bob,
A full house may win double.'*

'Housey-Housey'

We're outward bound for Singapore,
  And England's far behind us.
Old Jerry's subs are watching out,
  We'll catch it if they find us!
But now the 'Housey' cards are out,
  So just forget your trouble,
A single line wins thirty bob,
  A full house may win double.

I'm sea-sick as a blooming dog,
   I hate the raging billow.
Last night I thought my end had come
   As I lay on my pillow.
But see, the 'Housey' cards are out,
   And now the sergeant bellows,
'Eyes down, look in, full house this time,
   Come on, you lucky fellows!'

The CO had me on the mat
   At nine o'clock this morning.
He said my kit was in a mess
   And gave a friendly warning.
But now the 'Housey' cards are out
   It's 'Kelly's Eye', 'Blind Thirty',
'Top of the Shop', 'Ducks in a pond',
   What if the weather's dirty?

'Clickety-click' and 'forty-four',
   I've only one blank space now.
My pal, he needs a 'Number Nine',
   It's going to be a race now!
But Bill shouts 'House' and I am broke,
   My fags I'll have to borrow.
But if we're paid this afternoon,
   I'll play again tomorrow.

R. F. Palmer

Oh! Reykjavik!

We came from a land that was heaven
To a place far worse than hell,
They talk of their wonderful women
But we ain't met no Eskimo Nell.
Oh! Reykjavik! Oh! Reykjavik! Mush! Mush! Mush!

When we go out for some fun, sir,
We must all have a pass,
But the only hotel you're allowed in is
The one where you sit on your arse.
Oh! Reykjavik! *etc.*

Their homes are terribly pretty,
Surrounded by beautiful grass.
But when you dance with their women,
They throw you out on your arse.
Oh! Reykjavik! *etc.*

At Enugu, Gold Coast

We're a shower of bastards,
Bastards are we.
We're from Enugu,
The anus of the Empire and the British Army.
We're a shower of bastards,
Bastards are we.
We'd sooner fuck than fight for victory.

BLACK BOSOMS
'Bosoms, bosoms, bouncing bare,
Down the bush paths everywhere.'

Black Bosoms

Bosoms, bosoms, bouncing bare,
Down the bush paths everywhere,
What fantastic hand or eye,
Fashioned such dreadful symmetry.
Row on row of naked chests,
Glans Manalia, bosoms, breasts.
NAAFI teacups, lemon drops,
Bloodhound's ears, and razor strops.

Lagos Lagoon

In the year Anno Domini 1942,
In the city of Lagos there landed a crew.
They lived at the Grand and danced at the Ritz,
And amused themselves playing with native girls' tits.

  Lagos Lagoon, Lagos Lagoon,
  We're belting black velvet around Lagos Lagoon.

One night they went out to the native hot spots,
Pinching black udders and feeling black twats.
The fucking out there is easy, they say,
You can get a good grind for a piece of PK.

  Lagos Lagoon, *etc.*

They stayed there some while and in spite of the heat,
Refrained from inserting their sexual meat,
Till at last one night the whole crew got pissed,
And the native girls wiles could no longer resist.

  Lagos Lagoon, *etc.*

The WOP was the first one to leap into bed,
And quickly his arse winked a smart NGZ,
He found, when plugged in, there was plenty of clearance,
Reception was good, with fuck all interference.

  Lagos Lagoon, *etc.*

Of the two bad-type gunners the front was the first,
But a couple of stoppages marred a smart burst.
He got grit in his barrel though getting a stand,
And eased it down with a belt in the sand.

  Lagos Lagoon, *etc.*

The crew's navigator, his passions aflame,
Adjusted his bomb sights and took careful aim;
Getting red on red set, as he got the bint down,
He was wrong with his height and got red on brown.

    Lagos Lagoon, *etc.*

The number two pilot then came in to toil,
And without being told started pumping the oil;
He was quick on the draw, most reliable bloke,
And delivered the goods on the 48th stroke.

    Lagos Lagoon, *etc.*

The rear gunner's patience by waiting was marred,
And the size of the target made range-judgment hard;
The whole silhouette appeared to him strange,
And he fired all his ammo while well out of range.

    Lagos Lagoon, *etc.*

The others all finished, the skip went to town,
And made his approach, let everything down.
He found out by chance as he touched the earth
That he'd landed down wind, so he did soixante-neuf.

    Lagos Lagoon, *etc.*

In England at Moreton all went to the doc.,
And somewhat shamefacedly each showed him his cock.
He sent them to Halton, and now you will see,
The squadron's new markings – the letters VD.

    Lagos Lagoon, *etc.*

        The late S/Ldr Jimmy Sargeaunt, RAAF and RAF

A Note On Drumming And Bugling

Army drummers and buglers in the war memorised their duty calls by means of rhymes, of which these are examples.

The quarter hour – dress for parade:

You've got a face,
Like a chicken's arse.

Sick call:

Sixty-four, ninety-four,
He'll never go sick no more.
The poor fucker is dead.

Officers' dinner call:

The officers' wives get puddings and pies,
And sergeants' wives get skelly.
But privates' wives get fuck-all at all,
But hot cocks up their belly.

The guard salute:

Stand to attention, you raw-arsed recruit.
You've gone and made a fuck-up of the general salute.

5

Land
of Heat and Sweaty
Socks

SAYIDA BINT
'You're my little Gypo bint.'

For two and a half years the war was concentrated in the Middle East. Troopships from Australia, Britain, Canada, India, New Zealand and elsewhere converged there. By the end of 1940 Egypt had taken on almost the appearance of a huge army camp.

Mersa Matru, a tiny seaside village towards the Libyan border, swept by sandstorms for much of the year, and whose only previous claim to fame had been as the bathing place of Antony and Cleopatra, became a major centre of operations. For it was here that the railway ended, and the 'Blue' – the Western Desert – began. So it was to Matru that the weapons, ammunition and other supplies were brought and where they were stored, and there that the troops were assembled and despatched to the front.

My Little Dug-Out In The Sand

To the tune of George Formby's 'Standing at the Corner of the Street'

I'm a lousy, greasy gunner,
And I'm stationed at Matru,
And I have a little dug-out in the sand,
Where the fleas they play around me,
As I settle down at night,
In my flea-bound, bug-bound dug-out in Matru.

CHORUS
Where the floor is covered over with bully and meat loaf,
And the sand-bags let those howling blizzards through,
You can hear those fucking Eyeties as they circle round at night,
In my flea-bound, bug-bound dug-out in Matru.

Oh, I wish I had my girlie
To sit upon my knee,
To ease me of this awful pain I'm in,
And as much as I do love her,
How I wish that she were here –
In my flea-bound, bug-bound dug-out in Matru.

CHORUS

Sung by the Northumberland Fusiliers

In A Little Dug-Out

To the tune of 'Underneath the Arches'

In a little dug-out,
Way out upon the Blue,
In a little dug-out,
Ten miles south of Matru,
Every night you'll find me,
Tired out and worn,
Eating tins of bully,
And biscuits from night until the dawn,
Sleeping on some boxes,
A kit-bag for my head,
Fucking great big bombers overhead.
The toilet is a problem,
But the petrol does its work,
By a little dug-out,
Ten miles south of Matru.

Desert Blues

I'm just tired of seeing Eastern moons,
Bright red sunsets and the shining sand dunes.
Must get away,
I've got the desert blues.

Miles of sand whichever way I look,
Swell but only in a fairy tale book,
All I can say,
I've got the desert blues.

Camels galore, goats by the score,
Must go before it gets me down.
I never knew could be so blue,
Just take me to a respectable town.

I'm just tired of domes and minarets,
Eastern sunsets and the silhouettes,
Tired of it all,
I've got the desert blues.

The Song Of The 258 General Transport

The convoys of lorries moving men and supplies up into the desert were regularly strafed and bombed by Italian planes. Jarabub is an oasis to the west of Matru.

Now the 258 General Transport are out here,
They dash up and down the desert in top gear,
They have many punctures and back axles cracked,
But they're quickly repaired, that's the best of the Macks.
    Toodle-eh, Toodle-eh,
But they're quickly repaired, that's the best of the Macks.

One day on the desert while having some lunch,
The sergeant said, 'Now boys, I've got a hunch;
Supposing we grease all our nipples today,
It will help us run faster when we run away.'
    Toodle-eh, Toodle-eh,
It will help us run faster when we run away.

One day while out on the Jarabub run,
Three Eyeties dived at us from out of the sun,
Their bullets they whistled and whizzed through the air,
But where those bullets went there was nobody there.
    Toodle-eh, Toodle-eh,
But where those bullets went there was nobody there.

Now when we get back home in the pubs we will dive.
We'll tell them we're lucky to get back alive,
We'll talk of the things that we once used to do,
Such as pinching the tinned fruit from Mersa Matru.
        Toodle-eh, Toodle-eh,
Such as pinching the tinned fruit from Mersa Matru.

Side By Side

In September 1940 the Italians set out from Libya to capture Matru, but before they had got halfway, sat down to rest.

The days passed, and they showed no sign of moving on. Sir Archibald Wavell, Commander-in-Chief, Middle East, decided that if they wouldn't come and fight us, we should go and fight them. Thirty thousand soldiers set out to meet a force almost three times the size. The Italians, taken by surprise, ran for their lives.

To the tune of 'Side by Side'

Now, you've heard of Sir Archibald Wavell,
The man who made the Eyeties able,
Of running a mile,
In the Wooderson style,
    Side by side.

All through the heat of the summer,
We didn't worry at all,
They advanced on Sollum and Birrani
And were sure that Mersa would fall.
    Side by side.

As the Eyeties advanced on Birrani
With joy they nearly went barmy,
But they soon sobered up,
When we rounded them up,
    Side by side.

Oh, they got such a terrible headache,
They thought they'd been hit by an earthquake,
So they started to run,
Back the way they had come,
   Side by side.

Now they thought it was all over,
They didn't put up much of a fight,
They came out with their hands up,
And a little banner of white.
   Side by side.

So if ever you hear of an Eyetie,
Without palpitations you'll know why,
For they started to run,
Back the way they had come,
   Side by side.

Bardia Poem

The Italians fled back across the border and took refuge in the Libyan coastal fortress at Bardia. In January the ANZACs arrived at the gates with 22 Matilda tanks.

They took Bardia three days later, capturing 45,000 POWS, 462 artillery pieces and 129 tanks.

'Twas the show of the year, and the soldiers I hear
Were the fellows described as the best;
To the tune of the guns these grand ANZAC sons
Tore into battle with zest.

Now we all must agree that those sons of the free
Soon cleaned up that large bunch of wops.
Then to do the job right they sat down that night
To clean up his chianti and hops.

Till late in the night when they finished the fight,
They wined and talked over their task,
Until some silly fool, who liked his wine cool,
Shot a ·303 into the cask.

With a terrible boom that half wrecked the room
And blew the boys out through the door,
That cognac exploded like a shell overloaded,
And panicked the Eyeties once more.

Those Aussies were drunk from the wine they had sunk,
And they wouldn't strike matches for days.
Then they all made a vow, though they laugh at it now,
That in future it's temperance that pays.

There'll be battles much worse and they'll still drink and curse,
But a call brings them out on the run,
To the thick of the strife, when they'll fight for their life,
And stick to the last man and gun.

Ally Sloper's Cavalry

Even in the Middle East there were still plenty of soldiers far from where the action was; among them a unit of the Royal Army Service Corps, stationed on the Suez Canal.

They say old Britain's in a war,
Right bang up to the eyes,
With fighting men and women
On land and sea and skies.

But there's a bunch of soldiers
That are all forgot about.
For we're the old RASC –
They call us Ally Sloper's Cavalry.

The 'R' just stands for rations,
That all the troops require.
'A' is for ammunition
That you fire at Jerry men.

'S' stands for sausage,
And sugar for your tea.
And 'C' is for the comforts that you never get
In the bleeding RASC.

Now when this war is over,
Into Berlin we'll all go.
There'll be Hitler, Goering, Ribbentrop,
All there to watch the show.

Hitler unto Ribbentrop
Will say: 'What's that mob there?'
Ribbentrop will answer:
'I am guilty, oh mein herr.'

Ribbentrop will say, 'You see,
Why, that's the old RASC.
In the last world war,
They was very good to me.'

Then Hitler will say to Goebbels:
'I asked for information.
You never told me they
Had shock troops in the British nation.'

'Why we have taken the count,
It's quite plain to see,
I'd bargained for the army, navy, air force,
But forgot their RASC.'

B. Barnes

Egypt

To say that the British Empire's best did not hit it off very well with Egypt may be an understatement. The Egyptians themselves, who, while enjoying the economic boom created by the troops' presence, mostly had little reason to favour the Allied cause against the Axis one, were regarded as dirty and dishonest foreigners with a questionable right to be there at all. They were even held to blame by some of the British for their country's treacherous climate and terrain.

King Farouk himself, who did entertain pro-fascist sympathies at one time, and who was rumoured to be sending secret messages of encouragement to the enemy, was singled out for particular derision.

None the less, communication of some kind proved necessary with the natives. As these songs show, a kind of military pidgin Arabic emerged, which has enriched the English language with at least three colloquialisms – bint, shufti and berk.

Here is a brief glossary of the pidgin Arabic that appears in the songs that follow:

Anna Muskeen Mafeesh Fuloose – I've got
    no more money
Backsheesh – money
Bint – girl
Clifty – to thieve
Kam fuloose? – How much?
Mungaree bardin – Oh well, we'll eat
    tomorrow then
Quois keterre – very nice
Sayida – good day
Stanishwiya – wait a bit
Suffragi – servant
Talla heena – come here

The Suffragi's Wedding

I went to a Suffragi's wedding,
The Rhise and the Dhobi were there;
Of course I went on my camel,
All dressed up in fine camel hair.
Abdul Sayeed was the bridegroom,
His bride was a dusky young bint;
She cost him 300 piastres,
Less 1 mill because of her squint.
Oh, the camel bells were ringing,
And all the guests were singing,
T'was Quois Keterre,
From dawn to clear.
And so Keef Arlek,
Then we had some arrak,
Sayida, Sayida, Umbarrak,
For the sake of Auld Lang Syne.

Land Of Heat And Sweaty Socks

To the tune of 'There is a Tavern in the Town'

Land of heat and sweaty socks,
Sin and sand and lots of rocks,
Streets of sorrow, streets of fame,
Streets to which we give no name.

Streets of filth and stinking dogs,
Harlots, thieves and festering wogs,
Clouds of choking sand that blinds,
And drives poor airmen off their minds.

Aching hearts and stinking feet,
Gippo guts and camel meat.
The Arab's heaven – airmen's hell,
Land of Pharaohs – FARE THEE WELL.

Sayida Bint

I joined the Army
Not so long ago,
And they sent me
Out to Egypt right away.
At first I didn't like it,
I couldn't quench my thirst,
Till one day I started out to spoon.
Sayida bint,
I like your charming manner
To walk with you or talk with you
Would be my great desire;
Your charming little yashmak,
Your finger-tips of henna,
Make me say to other bints
Anna Muskeen Mafeesh Fuloose.
Two eyes of fire
That make me stand swire,
I'd give the world if I could call you dear.
But I think I'll call you Lena,
For it rhymes with Talla heena,
You're my little Gypo bint,
You're Quois keterre.

Shari Wag El Burka

To the tune of 'There is a Green Hill Far Away'

There is a street in Cairo, full of sin and shame.
Shari Wag El Burka is the bastard's name.

CHORUS
Russian, Greek and French bints, all around I see,
Shouting out: 'You stupid prick, abide with me.'

Two or three weeks later, when I see my dick,
Swiftly pack my small kit, and fall in with the sick.

   CHORUS

Five or six months later, free from sin and shame,
Back to the El Burka, just for fun and games.

   CHORUS

Alex On The Med

To the tune of 'The Mountains of Mourne'

Oh Mary, this Alex's a wonderful sight,
Where the wogs they all clifty by day and by night.
They'll polish your boots, and sell eggs and bread,
While we go for a swim in the beautiful Med.

We come here on leave from up in the Blue,
From Derna, Benghazi and Mersa Matru.
And Farouk, he comes out with a wave and a smile,
For the boys who are guarding his beautiful Nile.

King Farouk

This rude song about an unloved king arose from the resentment of soldiers visiting the Metro Cinema in Cairo at having to stand up for what was then the Egyptian national anthem, *Salaam Malik* (Salute to the King). They stood all right, but they sang their own words, not infrequently resulting in brawls with the local populace.

One story is that a group of drunken airmen, offered a lift back to their base from town one night, sang it throughout the journey. It was only when they arrived that they realised that the driver of the car in which they had been riding was King Farouk. It is said that he acted as a Good Chap and a Sport; though perhaps this was from fear of what they might do to him if he did not.

The second version, concerning Queen Farida, was introduced to relieve monotony.

To the tune of 'Salute to the King'

King Farouk, King Farouk,
Hang your bollocks on a hook,
Stanishwiya, pull your wire,
King Farouk Bardin.

CHORUS
He's the King of the Wogs,
He's the King of all the Wogs,
He's the King of the camels and the horses and the dogs,
He's the King of the plains where it never fucking rains,
Sayida, Queen Farida, Shufti Bint, Kam Fuloose.

Queen Farida's bright and gay,
'Cos she's in the family way,
Stanishwiya, pull your wire,
King Farouk Bardin.

CHORUS

Thanks For The Memory

To the tune of 'Thanks for the Memory'

Thanks for the memory, of the Berka and its bints,
The bootblack with the squints,
The bloke who's just down from the 'Blue'
His arm done up in splints,
How lovely it was.
Thanks for the memory, of camels and their humps,
Middle Eastern dumps,
Of Yankee beer that's far too dear, and gives us all the jumps,
How lovely it was.
Many's the time we've fretted
About cash at two-up we've betted,
But how in the Kiwi bar we've wetted,
We've drank wog beer with damn good cheer,
So thanks for the memory, of wog kids stabbing butts,
Eunuchs without nuts,
Of living in a country where we all got Gyppo guts.
Oh, thank you so much.

Queen Farida

To the tune of 'Salute to the King'

Queen Farida, Queen Farida,
How the boys would like to ride her,
Talla heena, quois keterre, mungaree bardin.

CHORUS

Queen Farida, give us backsheesh!
Queen Farida, give us backsheesh!
She's the queen of all the wogs,
Of all the jackals and the dogs,
Talla heena, quois keterre, mungaree bardin.

They're all brown bastards
And they dearly love their queen.
Talla heena, quois keterre, mungaree bardin.

CHORUS

Crete

In May 1941 we suffered one of our most stunning defeats of the war – the fall of Crete.

By that month, there were 28,600 Australian, British and New Zealand troops on the island. It was a formidable number; but many were tired and demoralised after their defeat on the Greek mainland; others were ill-trained and almost all were gravely under-equipped.

Churchill feared a German airborne attack, and urged major preparations to forestall it. General Freyberg, the commander, brusquely cabled the Prime Minister: 'Cannot understand nervousness. Am not in the least anxious about airborne attack.' He made his deployments on the conviction that the Germans would come by sea.

On 20 May 3,000 German paratroopers dropped in. They were quickly followed by 19,000 more, most of whom arrived by glider or troop air transport.

By the 26th, Freyberg cabled London that his position was 'hopeless . . . the limits of endurance have been reached by the troops under my command.'

As the Luftwaffe strafed them with impunity, our troops fled in almost total disarray towards the Royal Naval base in the south-west of Crete. Freyberg, trying to get up to the front to see what was happening there, was swept back by the crowds of panicking soldiers that filled the roads.

The Navy, at a cost of some 2,000 sailors' lives, managed to evacuate barely more than half the men – the claim made in the first song that 'We withdrew the majoritee', is strictly true, but only just. Over 14,000 were left behind. A handful escaped subsequently but most were killed and the rest taken prisoner.

The ANZAC troops, who mounted a last-ditch holding action in the area of Suda Bay to enable others to escape and who were among the last to withdraw, suffered particularly heavy casualties in relation to their numbers. These two songs commemorate two Australians who never made it. The second song, *Suda Bay*, became a favourite among British troops and was sent in by people from several parts of England.

Working In The Ordnance

To the tune of 'Waltzing Matilda'

Once a private soldier was sitting in his Ordnance Store
    Down by the shores of the Aegian Sea;
And he said when they asked him what he was a' doin' of,
    'I'm just a bloke in the AAOC.'

'Working in Ordnance, working in Ordnance,
    Handling the stores for the Infantree;
Trucks for your transport, uniforms to clothe you in,
    Fixing the guns for the Artilleree.'

Down came the Heinkels and down came the eighty-eights,
    Came down in thousands – one, two, three!
And they blasted the island, 'cos they owned the upper air,
    So we withdrew to a new countree.

Blew up our vehicles, ruined our Ordnance,
    Men – we withdrew the majoritee.
But the private stood while the transports were pulling out –
    'I'll always fight with the rearguard,' said he.

So the private soldier burnt down his Ordnance Store;
  Blew up his workshop with TNT,
And he smiled as he bent to buckle his equipment on –
  'I'll always fight with the rearguard,' said he!

'Fight with the rearguard – fight with the En Zeds –
  Fight with the men of the Sixth Divee.'
And his ghost may be heard round the seas where Ulysses sailed,
  He is the Pride of the AAOC.

Suda Bay

To the tune of 'Sulva Bay'

In an old Australian cottage,
With roses around the door,
A girl received a letter,
A letter from the war.

With her mother's arms around her,
She gave way to sobs and sighs.
And as she read that letter,
The tears fell from her eyes.

Why does she weep? Why should she cry?
Her boy's asleep so far away.
He played his part, that terrible day,
Now he lies asleep in Suda Bay.

Libya, Christmas 1940

Out in the Western Desert the Italians were still on the run. By the end of 1940 we had pushed them not only out of Egypt and East Africa but halfway across their colony, Libya, as well.

On Christmas Eve, the thoughts of 'Our Boys' turned homewards. They were not entirely kindly ones.

Hair on our shoulders, hair on our knees,
Bully beef and biscuits, over-ripe cheese,
Water that's salty and slimy too,
Sand in the sausages, sand in the stew.

Miles we have travelled, hours we have spent,
Roaming the desert, so weary and bent,
Stop here today, push on tomorrow,
We have nothing to spend, nothing to borrow.

Once we turned round and said, 'Thank God, at last.'
Then turned round again and returned twice as fast.
Arrived at our map ref. feeling like hell,
Six blokes missing, and the cookhouse as well.

Tomorrow is Christmas, how happy we'll be,
No beer, no fags – gee what a spree!
But our's is no hardship compared with the blokes
Camping in Blighty, away from their folks.

Why, even J. Priestley complained of their trials,
Far from a pub – at least fifteen miles.
So tomorrow we'll pray for the folks back home,
Far from their sweethearts and all, all alone.

That's solved our great problem – we know what to do.
We'll spend all our Christmas just praying for you.
But we'll say a wee prayer that some day you'll land
On this flee-ridden, bug-ridden stretch of sand.

DEUTSCHER, DEUTSCHER
'Saw a Jerry acting wary,
Thought I'd go and take a look.'

Then near-disaster struck in the form of Rommel and his Afrika Korps, who landed at Tripoli. By April 1941 we had been forced right back out of Libya, and Rommel was planning his victory dinner in Shepheard's Hotel in Cairo.

A single outpost of the British Empire held out in Libya – Tobruk. Here, the 'Desert Rats', British and ANZAC troops, remained under siege for eight long months before they were relieved. When they could, they crept out into the desert to harass the Afrika Korps.

Deutscher, Deutscher

To the tune of the German national anthem

Deutscher, Deutscher, über alles,
In the sands outside Tobruk,
Saw a Jerry acting wary,
Thought I'd go and take a look.

78

He was sitting, pants down, shitting,
Down a little shady pass.
Put a triflle up my rifle,
Aimed, and shot him up the arse.

There's A Tin Hat On My Bed

To the tune of 'There's a Bridle Hanging on the Wall'

For there's a tin hat hanging on my bed,
And a bomber flying overhead.
There's a lot of prayer books being read,
And a lot of curses being said.

There's a searchlight shining in the sky,
And the ack-ack shells begin to fly.
But that Dago bomber's up so high,
I think that someone's going to die.

Though I've heard that hits are few,
Somehow I knew 'twould be me.
I waited for that bomb to blow,
When it burst beneath my nose.
I found I suddenly rose,
And went where the good soldiers go.

Oh! Fucking Tobruk

A song similar to that which commemorated Halkirk (see page 44) was written by an Australian during the siege.

> All fucking fleas, no fucking beer,
> No fucking booze since we've been here.
> And will it come? No fucking fear,
> In fucking Tobruk.
>
> The fucking rumours make me smile.
> The fucking wogs are fucking vile.
> The fucking pommies cramp your style,
> In fucking Tobruk.
>
> All fucking dust, no fucking rain,
> All fucking fighting since we came,
> This army's just a fucking shame,
> In fucking Tobruk.
>
> The bully makes me fucking wild,
> I'd nearly eat a fucking child,
> The salt water makes me fucking riled,
> In fucking Tobruk.
>
> Air raids all day and fucking night,
> Huns striving with all fucking might.
> They give us all a fucking fright
> In fucking Tobruk.
>
> Best fucking place is fucking bed,
> With blanket over fucking head.
> And then they think you're fucking dead,
> In fucking Tobruk.

Tobruk Song

Because I'm fucked off, fucked off,
Fucked off as can be,
Fucked off, fucked off, fucked off lads are we.
And when this war is over,
And once again I'm free,
There'll be no more fucking soldiering for me.

Ali Baba Morshead And His Twenty Thousand Thieves

A popular entertainment in Tobruk, indeed throughout the 'Middle East Theatre' was listening to Lord Haw-Haw's nightly broadcasts to the allied forces, beamed from Nazi-occupied Belgrade every evening from 9.30 to 10.00 p.m.

Hearing his snide insults against them did wonders for their morale. They delighted particularly in the nick-names he thought up for them, the most famous of which was, of course, 'Desert Rats'. Another Haw-Haw-ism that stuck was his description of the Australian forces under General Leslie Morshead as 'Ali Baba Morshead and his 20,000 thieves'.

Old Jerry had us on the run – the news was far from hot.
He had his foot in Egypt, and the Sphinx was on the spot.
The GOC, despondent, sent signals out in sheaves,
To Ali Baba Morshead and his 20,000 thieves.

So Leslie called his G. staff and whispered in their ears.
His message went to Auky – 'Have a pot and drown your fears.
We'll make that bastard Rommel think he's got the Gippo heaves,
Will Ali Baba Morshead and his 20,000 thieves.'

So we travelled down to Egypt from these pleasant lands afar,
We knew the need was urgent 'cause we'd come by motor car.
We didn't stop in Cairo, and Alexandria grieves
O'er Ali Baba Morshead and his 20,000 thieves.

Now Rommel's got a headache, his tanks can't take a trip,
His dropshots aren't so wonderful, his air force makes you sick.
His glorious dreams of yesterday are ditched, and is he peeved!
While Ali Baba gloats over his 20,000 thieves.

Will history repeat itself, now we're once more in the game?
Will the form displayed in '41 this year be the same?
If so, then Rommel's stonkered, when o'er the plan he weaves,
'Gainst Ali Baba Morshead and his 20,000 thieves.

By an A.I.F. signaller, Western Desert

The Harasser's Song

Lord Haw-Haw described the 450 Australian Air Force as 'The Desert
Fighter-Bomber Squadron of the Royal Harassers'.

To the tune of 'White Horse Inn'

Raise up your glasses and drink Harassers,
We're taking the air at first light,
To fly in Rommel's direction
To bomb and lay off deflection.
And when the war is a memory
The Desert Harassers will be
A name they'll always remember.
So drink to four-fifty with me.
Dadada. Bombom.

From Alamein to the USA,
From Perth to the Outer Barcoo,
From near and far we will struggle
To join once more in the gaggle.
The years roll past, and you're clapped, at last;
But in the desert, at home or at sea,
You'll always be a Harasser,
So drink to four-fifty with me.

Sgt-Pilot Devon Minchin

Rats Of Tobruk

'Good morning, Rats,' the donkey brayed,
'Rats at the end of your tether.
I hear your nerves are somewhat frayed,
Shall I snap them altogether?'
   Hee-Haw, Hee-Haw, I'll snap them altogether.

And he called to the birds of prey,
'Swoop low on the British Rats;
They're afraid of the light of day,
They live in caves like bats.'
   Hee-Haw, Hee-Haw, they live in holes – the Rats.

So the vultures flocked for the kill,
And they dived on the hospital ships,
And the hospital high on the hill,
They blew the wards to bits.
   Wh-e-e-e Cr-r-ump, they blew sick men to bits.

Then in the fortress drear,
Which they wouldn't evacuate,
The Rats began to stir –
The British are slow to hate.
   Rat-a-tat, Rat-a-tat, the Rats sat down to hate.

Full gorged with easy game,
The vultures flocked once more,
A hundred plus they came,
And dived on the shattered shore.
    Eeee-ow, Eeee-ow, they dived and rose no more.

Crash went the big ack-ack,
Ker-plonk went the Bofors guns,
And the little Rats stood back,
And spat at the hateful Huns.
    Rat-a-tat, Rat-a-tat, spat lead at the hated Huns.

The Rats gave a grin to themselves,
And they worked as they'd always done,
Worked in the dark like elves,
Unseen by anyone.

The Dock Rats swarmed on the gallant ships
And carried the cargoes away,
Food, ammunition, tanks and guns,
Safe hid by the break of day.

Safe hid and passed to the Desert Rats
Who guard the outer wire,
(And what if we did pinch some of the beer,
A Rat is worth his hire.)

And the Desert Rats gnawed at his lines by night
Creeping up on the Huns like ghosts,
Till he screamed and broke in panic flight,
And we took his hard-pressed posts.

In the grey little country over the sea,
The Bulldog cocked his eye,
'Well done, you Rats of Tobruk,' he said.
'We hang on, you and I.'

The Conchie

A 'conchie' was a conscientious objector – a man who refused to bear arms on religious grounds.

He came to the depot a figure of shame,
    A 'conchie' refusing to fight,
Who said 'twas no glory to kill and to maim,
    To see who was wrong and who right!

We thought it a slight on the Medical Corps
    When they drafted the 'conchie' to us,
And thought it an insult that in time of war,
    A soldier should make so much fuss.

We called him a coward and laughed him to scorn,
    Each evening when he knelt to pray,
We said he was yellow and should have been born
    As a woman, but nought would he say.

In the African desert one hot August day,
    When the fighting was heavy and grim,
A messenger came from headquarters to say,
    That our chance of survival was dim.

When darkness descended our stretchers we took
    To bring in the wounded and slain.
Tho' Jerry was shelling, by hook or by crook
    We went out again and again.

At last when we'd finished our task for the night
    We reported and answered our roll,
The 'conchie' was absent. We guessed that in fright,
    He'd bolted and missed the recall.

Another day passed in the tropical heat
    And when the sun sank in the west,
Another six miles we'd been forced to retreat
    And the enemy gave us no rest.

As we lay under cover the following night
    And stared out across 'No Man's Land',
We saw in the glare of a stray Verey Light
    Two men creeping in, hand-in-hand.

The 'conchie' 'd returned. He was wounded and worn,
    And was leading a man who was blind,
His face was blood-spattered, his clothing was torn,
    And his leg dragging useless behind.

All day he had tended the shell-blinded man
    In the glare of the African sun,
And as darkness fell the long journey began,
    And collapsed in our lines when 'twas done.

Our 'conchie' now wears a VC on his breast,
    We call him a coward no more.
He still says his prayers e'er going to rest,
    The pride of the Medical Corps.

R. F. Palmer

Lili Marlene

There was one regular item on the Nazi broadcasts to British troops that the latter did not scoff at – the playing of the record of Lala Andersen singing *Lili Marlene*, at 9.57 p.m. every night.

It is, perhaps, the most popular soldiers' song ever. Throughout the Vietnam war, it was played through loudspeakers at Travis Air Force Base, San Francisco, to troops embarking for and returning from Vietnam. It has been adopted by the Canadian Infantry as its official marching song; and in 1971 it topped the Japanese hit parade.

Before World War II it was virtually unknown. It had been written by a German private in World War I, Hans Liep, in honour, not as is commonly assumed, of one girl but two – Lili and Marlene, who used to wait for him in the evenings, underneath the lamplight across the barrack square.

It was set to music by Norbert Schutzer, but rejected by over thirty German music publishers and record companies until Lala Andersen took it up.

In World War II the German forces' broadcasting service began playing it regularly to Nazi soldiers abroad, and it became a firm and lasting favourite with them.

Its impact on the British forces was just as great. Veterans I have spoken to, who did not hear it on the radio, recall listening to it wafting over from the enemy lines in the desert, or sung by German POWs as they were marched to the camps. It seemed that everyone was immediately captivated by it – even before they knew what the words were.

There were stories of the British and the Germans moving into battle against one another, both singing *Lili Marlene*. There was a German rumour that at El Alamein, the 51st Highland Division launched an attack in the hope of capturing a copy of the record. Later, it was claimed that both sides would sometimes cease firing a little before ten o'clock at night, and resume shortly afterwards, so that they could hear it on the radio.

Inevitably, the British and the ANZACs set words of their own to the tune. It was said that when Hitler learnt about this, he 'flew into a towering rage, and reported it as a flagrant breach of the Geneva Convention'. It is certainly the case that Dr Goebbels ordered the Nazi radio station in Belgrade to stop playing it in their broadcasts to British troops. (The director obeyed for a few days, and then resumed playing it again 'by mistake'.)

Another story about the effect of *Lili Marlene* comes from later in the war, after the invasion of Italy. E. L. writes: 'Somewhere in the middle of Italy below Florence our regiment was in action, but only technically so; we were anti-tank gunners and our guns were in position to support the infantry, but there was very little going on . . .

'On one particular very dark night the position was fluid, as the radio announcers used to say. It was a lush part of the country and there was plenty of vino to be had. A small party of German soldiers had been drinking in some little café on their side of the line and when they had had enough and decided to go, they linked arms and lurched off along the road in what they believed to be the direction of their billet . . .

'It seemed a terrible long way, but after several rests, they heard the strains of *Lili Marlene* coming from a building by the side of the road. They burst in, convinced that they were among friends at last, only to find that they were in our regimental cookhouse, where our cooks were having a bit of a party. They were duly put in the bag.'

The Dive Bombers' Song

In North Africa, one of the early anti-German songs set to the tune of *Lili Marlene* was written by an Australian with 450 Fighter-Bomber Squadron, 239 Wing, in riposte to Haw-Haw's 'regrets' for the 'dreadful losses they have suffered'.

To the tune of 'Lili Marlene'

Get the right deflection,
Check reflector sight,
Give your speed correction,
And see your range is right.
Then you can press the tit, old son,
And blow the Hun to kingdom come,
Poor Marlene's boy-friend will
Never see Marlene.

Half a thousand pounds of
Anti-personnel,
Half a dozen rounds of
The stuff that gives them hell.
Finish your bomb dive, zoom away,
And live to fight another day.
But poor Marlene's boy-friend will
Never see Marlene.

Belching ammunition,
Petrol truck ahead,
Glorious conditions
For filling them with lead.
Finish your bomb dive, zoom away,
And live to fight another day.
Then poor Marlene's boy-friend will
Never see Marlene.

The Party At El Alamein

Now you've all heard the story of Churchill's cigar,
And most of you've shuftied a native bazaar,
But the story I'll tell you, you'll know is quite true,
How Field Marshal Rommel was stopped up the Blue.

Tally ho, Tally ho, and that was as far as the bastard did go!

When first he got started he had all the luck,
He captured Birrani and then took Tobruk,
And the boys were amazed at him doing so well,
For he swore he would dine at the Shepheard's Hotel.

Tally ho, Tally ho, *etc.*

While back in Berlin they shouted with glee,
When Goebbels gave word of the great victory,
He told them all stories of what he had seen,
But fuck all a word about El Alamein.

Tally ho, Tally ho, *etc.*

Now along came the Nazis, the Eyeties as well,
And that was the day that we blew them to hell,
For the answer to the Panzer while up in the Blue,
Was a twenty-five pounder and a Bofor or two.

Tally ho, Tally ho, *etc.*

Now right into Alex; they thought they were sure,
But we could have told them their chances were poor,
For shoulder to shoulder at Alamein box,
Stood the Aussies, the Kiwis, the Tommies and Jocks.

Tally ho, Tally ho, *etc.*

Now the Highland Division went in with the steel,
And the Nazis, the bastards, they started to squeal,
We took thousands of prisoners and tanks by the score,
And that was the end of the Afrika Korps.

Tally ho, Tally ho, *etc.*

When all this is over back home you will soar,
Rush into civvies and soldier no more,
And the people will ask you 'Oh where have you been?'
Just tell them to a party at El Alamein.

Tally ho, Tally ho, *etc.*

Down By El Alamein

One night in the desert 'twas calm and serene,
Our troops moving up in an endless stream.
The barrage was set for ten p.m.,
Down by El Alamein.

Our guns opened fire again and again.
Our objectives were taken by nine a.m.,
The Afrika Korps will rest no more,
Down by El Alamein.

Now when this war is over, and victory is won,
And gunners are gunners no more,
They'll think of the desert for many a day,
Of the Black Watch, the Gordons with us in the fray,
Of the Highland Division who chased Rommel away,
Away from El Alamein.

A Gunner of the Royal Artillery,
51st Highland Division, from Arbroath

The Rifles, The Skins And The Bold Fusiliers

This, an adaptation of a traditional Ulster song, commemorates one of the great turning points of the war – the final rout of the Afrika Korps after over three years of bitter fighting. The capture of Tunisia in the spring of 1943 cleared the way for the invasion of Nazi-occupied Europe a few months later, and also resulted in vast numbers of German soldiers and equipment being taken.

The Irish Rifles, the Irish Guards and the Irish Fusiliers were involved in one of the key battles – the capture of the German strongholds in the mountains north of Medjez-el-Bab, by the Algerian–Tunisian border. Longstop Hill, as the troops called it, was described by Alan Morehead as 'darker than the surrounding country and more sinister, a great two-humped bulk that heaved itself out of the wheatfields'. Dominating the plain that led to Tunis, it was for both sides the symbol of pre-eminence.

The Allied assault continued for more than three days. Some of our men fought for forty-eight hours without a break before collapsing from physical and nervous exhaustion. But they captured it.

They then moved quickly across the plain to Tunis where, to their astonishment, they were resisted by only a handful of snipers, and greeted by great, cheering crowds of French who festooned them with flowers.

To the tune of 'The Mountains of Mourne'

When the war drums had sounded the clans to the call,
Three brave Irish Regiments were there on the ball,
Defenders of Ulster, right down through the years,
The Rifles, the Skins and the Bold Fusiliers.

They landed in Africa to clash with the Hun,
And came out in good time to miss none of the fun,
They jumped into action with three hearty cheers,
Did the Rifles, the Skins and the Bold Fusiliers.

Haw-Haw is a liar, a truth you'll admit,
He said that our lads were not doing their bit,
But they'll dash Hitler's hopes and they'll crown Goering's fears,
Will the Rifles, the Skins and the Bold Fusiliers.

A tanner war-pay is not much you'll admit,
But it helps all the lads out here doing their bit,
It helps to buy fags and a few extra beers,
For the Rifles, the Skins and the Bold Fusiliers.

'Twas the week before Easter the enemy had
Great fighting positions north of Medjez-el-Bab,
But without hesitation and nothing to fear,
Were the Rifles, the Skins and the Bold Fusiliers.

On the hills called Tangoucha they opened their show,
And soon from that hill Jerry quickly did go,
They hoisted the white flag through their deadly fears
Of the Rifles, the Skins and the Bold Fusiliers.

When Longstop had fallen we knew we'd have fun,
To the plains with our rifles we followed the Hun,
When we marched into Tunis, the French gave three cheers,
For the Rifles, the Skins and the Bold Fusiliers.

As we marched in through Tunis heading straight for Cap Bon,
The French in their thousands cried *'Les Anglais, tres bon'*,
They cried with delight, all the women in tears,
To see the Rifles, the Skins and the Bold Fusiliers.

W. G. Wood

Where The Hun Is, We Go

With the capture of Tunis, Cap Bon and Bizerta, the war in Africa was over, and preparations began for the invasion of Europe.

'At this time,' writes Alex Grant, who was with the 121 Field Regiment, Royal Artillery, 'our little drink-ups – and believe me they were little owing to Montgomery's strict ideas on drink – Gunner Murray used to stand and recite this poem to the lads. His Scottish twang was a treat to listen to. One of our pals, Ted Sharpe, christened Jock Murray "Thrushy", owing to his melodious twang.

'This poem will be remembered by the lads from Leeds, and also by many Londoners who were recruited as "extras" just after El Alamein. Though not strictly a song, they way Jock recited it, it was almost a song.'

How warm beat the sun from this African sky,
As we worked on the guns day by day,
With half of our mind on the job in hand,
And the other half far away,
In the land we love, with the folks we love,
For whom we work and fight,
And we think of them still while on sentry go,
In the star-shine of the night.

We have harried the Hun 'neath this sweltering sun,
From this land of a thousand pests,
Its verminous breed, its scorpions, ants,
Mosquitoes and all the rest.
Then our home was the gunpit and sand-walled trench,
And our bed was that self-same sand.
Sand was our outlook all about,
For such is this desolate land.

Yet the Hun fights on in other lands,
And where the Hun is, we'll go,
Whilst the threat of Might overshadows Right,
So long as the Hun is our foe.
Even now, like a breaking summer's day,
E'er the sun has topped the hill,
The light of Victory gently glows,
And the dews of hope distil.

Yet the final battle must be fought,
And many a fighting man must die.
The darkness of sorrow o'er many a home,
In many a heart shall lie.
Let your hearts be meantime, bright with hope,
Have faith in the Right and us,
And if you are given to prayer, my friend,
Then pray ye somewhat thus:

Lord bless our sons who fight Thy cause,
In body and soul them bless.
Bless Thou the arms with which they fight,
And crown them with success,
That the torch may be in their hands relit,
Freedom born again,
Fraternity among freedom kind,
So be it Thy will.

Gunner James Murray,
276 Battery, 121 Field Regiment, R.A.

The Second A.I.F.

To the tune of 'Far Away'

I'll sing a song of fellows
Who made their country's name,
Who taught the world that freedom
Was not a thing of shame.

They joined the second A.I.F.,
A happy bunch of blokes,
And they marched and trained and marched and trained all day.
Their embarkation orders came,
They marched down to the ship,
And sailed and sailed and sailed and sailed away.

Far away – far away,
But you can bet your life that they'll
Be coming back some day.

They landed on a foreign shore and camped out in the sun,
And they lived and ate and slept and breathed in dust
Then they marched out on the desert,
Got the Eyeties on the run,
For their orders were to win the war or bust.

Far away – far away,
But you can bet your life that they'll
Be coming back some day.

They spoilt a half-baked Caesar's plans,
And cooked old Hitler's goose,
When they fought and fought and fought with might and main,
Then they marched back to the ship once more
Glad their job was done,
And they sailed and sailed and sailed back home again.

Far away – far away,
And you can bet your life that they'd been
Waiting for that day.

So drink a toast to all these lads
On land and air and sea,
They did their bit to keep old Aussie's flag flying free.

Far away – far away,
But you can bet your life that they'll
Be coming back some day.

6

Patriotic Poetesses

THE SONG OF THE LAGOS BAR-GIRLS
'Me no jigajig for you no more.'

Back home, a host of lady patriots were penning noble sentiments about 'The Boys' that contrast somewhat with the songs the boys were singing.

The first one was sent by its authoress to Montgomery, during the battle of El Alamein. She still has the acknowledgment she received from a staff officer.

Who Said Decadent England?

To a Salvation Army tune

Who said decadent England,
Who said lazy and soft?
Who thought us ready for throwing
Into the Axis melting pot?
We'll show them just how mistaken
Such wishful thoughts turn out,
When together with our allies
We shall turn things
Into a final German, Jap and Eyetie rout.

The Motherland

Sung in an air-raid shelter in Tooting.

It is the dear old land, is the Motherland,
And when she sounds the call,
Her boys in other, far-off lands
Obey it one and all.
It's every Briton's duty to do what he can do
To defend the British Empire,
To stand and see her through.

It is the dear old land, is the Motherland,
Her sons are ever true.
Her boys in other far-off lands
Will see her through and through.
She's as good as in days of yore.
We are ready, aye and steady,
Whilst the British Bulldog's
Watching at the door.

The Bootle Air-Raid Shelter Song

Mrs Mary van Eker writes: 'I was but a civilian who ran to the air-raid shelter every time the alert sounded. There was no author to this song really, someone sang a line and then someone sang another. It comes spontaneous to us here.'

To the tune of 'Trees'

I know that I will live to see
The victory over Germany.
The Motherland will have her way,
For her the sun will shine one day,
A million happy lips will say,
'To Thee dear Lord did we not pray.'
And when the battle has been won,
We'll think of those who have passed on.
Did they not die that we'd be free,
Like Jesus did on Calvary.
Then I shall die most peacefully,
Knowing that British soil is free.

The Song Of The Lagos Bar-Girls

Me no likee English soldier.
Yankee soldier come ashore.
Yankee soldier plenty money.
Me no jigajig for you no more.

Give Thanks In Everything

One dreary morning, found
A tiny text from some child's book
Wet, lying on the ground.
Haphazardly, I read:
'Give thanks in everything,'
This rain-soaked fragment said.
How stupid! mused my dreary mind,
There's War and Death and Fear!
It seemed while dwelling on this theme,
This oddest text brought cheer.
The chaos of our war-torn towns,
The loss, uprooted way of lives,
And children playful even so,
By lonely fearful wives.
So give thanks for everything,
Yes, though with us death and fear,
Come, send your cheery laughs and quips,
To our men who are not here.

Mrs Bessie Cockburn,
Birkenhead, 1943

Tom Blamey's Boys

A remarkable practitioner of this genre was 'The Durban Signaller', alias Mrs Edith Campbell of Pietermaritzburg in Natal, South Africa.

During the war, Edith devoted herself to providing a home-from-home for Australian servicemen and merchant seamen who passed through, and even re- named her house 'Little Australia'. In her spare time she wrote songs to sing to her visitors when they arrived.

Tom Blamey was C-in-C of the Australian forces in World War II. A 'Ginger Mick' is a good kind of digger. 'MN' is a contraction for 'Merchant Navy'.

To the tune of 'Advance Australia Fair'

Tom Blamey's boys are in the breach
　　For good King George's realm,
The Empire has no cause for fear,
　　With Blamey at the helm;
His are the shock-troops of the world,
　　They stand superb, supreme,
They're rushed to every danger point;
　　They are the Huns' bad dream.

And what they'll do – 'twill be a sin – to Adolf in Berlin!

We blame the Huns, for they're to blame,
　　We've warned them, but they're deaf;
So wait till Blamey blames them next,
　　With his great A.I.F.,
Who've walloped Musso's Woppies,
　　And they won't be to blame,
If what they do to the Gestapo
　　Isn't just a shame!

Tom Blamey's boys will have their spin – Goreblameying Berlin!

We've heard of going berserk, boys,
　　We've heard of going wild,
But wait till 'Ginger Mick' and Bill
　　(Who wouldn't hurt a child,
Nor any girl or woman –
　　These they put upon a throne
Just as they do the mothers, wives,
　　And sisters of their own).

Get going into Hitler's skin with bayonets in Berlin!

Tom Blamey down to 'Ginger Mick',
　　And all the ranks between,
They mean just what they swear they mean,
　　And swear just what they mean;
They're out to blast the blinking Hun
　　And it won't be their fault,
If they do not make Berchtesgaden,
　　Turn a somersault!

Gorblimey! Wait till 'Mick' starts in Goreblameying Berlin!

There'll Always Be An England
While Australia Will Be There

To the tune of 'There'll Always be an England'

I give you a health
'Lads of the Commonwealth!'
The sons of the breed,
And the true ANZAC creed;
Across the world their thousands speed
To help old England in her need –
They come in their young strength to bring
Fresh hope and cheer which makes us sing:

There'll always be an England
   While Australia will be there,
There'll always be blue skies above
   While 'Cobbers' clear the air.
There'll always be an Empire
   While Diggers bayonets flash,
In vanguards of the shock troops
   Ever thirsting for a clash.

Star-spangled flag –
Flag that will never sag
To Wop or Hun
The 'Rising Sun'
Will never set.
The NZ's too –
Sons of the ANZACs who
Won deathless fame,
And their brave name
By Diggers shared.

There'll always be an Empire
   And England shall be free
So long as 'Ginger Mick' is what
   He always used to be!

The Durban Signaller

Mother's Song

In pubs in the north of England many women sang a different style of song:

I never raised my boy
   To be a soldier.
I brought him up to be
   My pride and joy.
Who dare to lay a gun
   Upon his shoulder,
And teach him how to kill
   Another mother's boy?

I never raised my boy
   To be a soldier.
I brought him up to stay
   At home with me.
There would be no war today,
   If every mother would say,
I never raised my boy
   To be a soldier.

A Child's Prayer

God bless my soldier Daddy,
To the war he had to go,
Take care of him while fighting,
Because I love him so.

God let my prayer be answered,
Don't let me pray in vain,
God bless my soldier Daddy,
And bring him safe home again.

7

Allies
(We Don't Think)

GAS ALERT
'... *worse by far*
Are the fumes that blow
Around the Kiwi bar!'

The Old Transvaal

The South Africans were bitterly criticised for their part in Operation Crusader, launched in November 1941, to relieve the besieged Tobruk garrison.

Major-General Pienaar seems first to have misunderstood orders to throw his troops into battle in support of the New Zealanders, and dithered for some thirty-six hours. He then sent in a single battalion, but when it came under shell-fire, told it to return.

Visited that night by two extremely insistent New Zealand officers, Pienaar agreed to move into action the next day; but was again the last to move.

Meanwhile, the forces responsible for trying to break out of Tobruk waited in vain for him to get close enough to meet up with him. In their fury, they blamed on Pienaar the failure of the whole exercise.

There's a thousand fucking bastards in the Old Transvaal,
And not a bloody one in Tobruk;
When Jerry brought his guns up, for the big attack,
The SA boys all took their fucking hook.
So take me back to the Old Transvaal,
That's where I long to be.

The Battle For Fondouk Gap

Often criticised unfairly for their alleged 'softness', the Americans did, though, put up a rather dubious performance at the battle for Fondouk Gap in Tunisia in April 1943. As this sarcastic song shows, the reaction of their British comrades-in-arms was less than forgiving.

Alexander's aim was to cut off Rommel's retreat and stop the Afrika Korps from re-forming to launch a new offensive. He entrusted it to the 9th Corps of the First Army, composed of the British 6th Armoured Division, an infantry brigade of the 46th Division and the US 34th Infantry Division.

The infantry's objective was to capture the heights on either side of the gap to allow the tanks to pass through. The attack was to start on the night of 7–8 April. Inexplicably, the Americans were almost three hours late in starting, and the crucially important cover of darkness was lost.

As they came under enemy fire, the Americans simply halted and took cover. Their failure to press home their attack allowed the Germans to turn almost all their fire-power on to the British, who had already been suffering 'moderate-to-heavy' casualties (to use the army public relations officers' jargon) but who had been making determined progress. Thus the odds were turned impossibly against them.

Faced with this fiasco, General Crocker – in command – decided that the tanks would have to pass through all the same, unless total disaster was to result. The men of the British 6th drove their vehicles straight over the minefields and right at fifteen anti-tank guns covering the narrow gap. Thirty-four tanks were knocked out and sixty-seven men killed.

Our Cousins

To the tune of 'Miss Otis Regrets . . .'

Our cousins report the objective is clear today, General.
Our cousins regret they're unable to stay today.
For the Germans are giving them *hell*,
And one of their soldiers is feeling rather unwell, General.
Our cousins regret they're unable to play today.

When we woke up to find that the pass was still firmly held, General.
We sent an LO to encourage them in the fray.
But our cousins had gone to ground,
'Cause the noise of the battle was such a goddam sound, General.
Our cousins regret they're unable to fight today.

So the armour went through and fanned out on the plain, General.
Leaving the price that they'd had to pay.
But Sherman tanks are US made
And Kairouan was therefore taken by the Yanks, General.
And the papers all said that our cousins had won the day.

Gas Alert

I've diced with death and
   smelt his foetid breath
But let me tell you Dig
   that worse by far
Are the fumes that blow
   around the Kiwi bar!

Cairo, August 1942

8

Frightfully
G.H.Q.

VENAL VERA
'While his mind's on copulation I'm exacting information.'

Few species were held in greater disdain than staff officers – those frightfully well-spoken, well-turned-out gents who never actually did any fighting.

'A' Lighters

' "A" Lighters' was the code name given for tank landing craft, while they were still on the secret list.

The RNVR crews who manned them in Egypt, ferrying tanks from Alexandria along the sub-infested coast to Mersa Matru, were honoured for their bravery by Montgomery, who conferred on them the right to wear the '8' (for 8th Army) insignia on the Africa Star ribbons.

To be declaimed in the manner of Stanley Holloway

There's a famous seaside place called Mersa Matru,
That's noted for heaven knows what.
But said C-in-C Med as he poured o'er his charts
'Ee, that's just blooming spot.'

'We'll send "A" Lighters to Mersa Matru,'
Said C-in-C Med to his staff.
'So make all arrangements for comforts for lads,
Give 'em feather beds, booze and a bath.'

So straightway staff left Sir Archie
To do as their Admiral 'ad bid,
Till commander chap what's in charge of staff said,
'Nay, let's have a pink gin instead.'

From Maxims they went to the Union,
From the Union to Pastroudi's Grill,
And they haven't been seen from that day to this,
I expect they are boozing there still.

Now when 'A' Lighter chaps get up to Mersa Matru,
In response to their Admiral's call,
They find no feather beds, no booze and no bath,
In fact they find sweet bugger all.

So poor officer chap what's in charge of base
Sent signals by air, sea and land.
But said C-in-C Med: 'Ee, that's all right –
My staff 'ave matter in 'and.'

But staff as we know are still on the booze,
And it's no use to grumble or shout,
'Cause there'll be no comforts in Mersa Matru
Till pink gin in Alex runs out.

S/Lt L. C. Bonning, RNVR

Frightfully G.H.Q.

This double-act was a great hit at 'Sods' Operas', as troop-concerts were known.

To be sung in the manner of the Weston Brothers

We're Bulwarks of Britain out here in the East,
We're fighting the fight of the true,
As we bravely attack in the Battle of Bumph,
We're frightfully G.H.Q.

1. I'm Staff-Captain Cholmondely – I'm Eton and Ox.
   The blood in my veins runs blue.
   My Colonel and Pater both hunted the fox –
   We're frightfully G.H.Q.

2. I'm Staff-Captain Ponsonby – 'Lords', and all that.
   My Major, God bless 'im, is too.
   They gave me three pips 'cause I played a straight bat,
   We're frightfully G.H.Q.

And now up in Cairo we sweat and we toil,
Determined to see the show through;
As we totter in taxis from Groppi's to Doll's –
We're frightfully G.H.Q.

We asked to be sent to the Blue for a year;
The Colonel's reply wasn't clear –
He said that he thought we'd do less harm down here.
We're frightfully G.H.Q.

When Rommel advanced by desert and track,
We hoped we might meet at Gezira, then 'crack';
By sheer weight of numbers we'd've turned the cad back.
We're frightfully G.H.Q.

But 'Full Aid to Russia' they're crying today,
We're in favour of sending a lot Stalin's way,
But no membership cards for Gezira, we pray.
We're frightfully G.H.Q.

Yet we're quite democratic. For freedom we thirst.
Why, we know a young Private – a Waaf named Hearst.
Between you and me she's expecting her first.
We're frightfully G.H.Q.

         (Quiet, Cads – stripes we mean.)

We asked a Staff Sergeant we'd always thought shy
What 'Q' did with so many copies, and why?
But we honestly cannot believe his reply,
For we're frightfully G.H.Q.

We've heard of Free French but we cannot agree.
Since we visited Shepheard's, between you and me,
We've not found a Frenchwoman yet who's buckshee.
We're frightfully G.H.Q.

There's no doubt at all, Lady Astor would say,
That united effort will carry the day;
But change our red arm-bands for yellow – oh nay;
We're frightfully G.H.Q.

We really know nothing of tactics of war.
We much prefer *Film Fun* to George Bernard Shaw,
So they're posting us to the Intelligence Corps.
We're frightfully G.H.Q.

For King and for Empire we're ready to die;
The horrors of war we've faced without cry.
We've even drunk cups of what NAAFI calls 'chai'.
We're frightfully G.H.Q.

Nothing defeats us. We'll both make our mark.
When we want some advice and we're both in the dark,
We don't let the side down – we ask the Chief Clerk –
We're frightfully G.H.Q.

Venal Vera

Though confirmation has not been forthcoming, it is said that Quentin Reynolds, the famous Canadian radio war correspondent, composed *Venal Vera* at the request of British security officials in Cairo.

They were apparently concerned with how freely staff officers talked to the Cairene tarts while on the booze. Most of the latter were not Egyptians, and it is said that the social sophistication, poise and beauty of some were such as to suggest that they might not have been tarts either.

The alleged purpose of the song was to warn officers to keep their mouths shut, whatever else they did. But its greatest popularity was, of course, in the non-commissioned ranks, as an anti-officer song.

To the tune of 'The Foggy, Foggy Dew'

They call me Venal Vera, I'm a lovely from Gezira,
The Führer pays me well for what I do.
The order of the battle, I obtained from last night's rattle
On the golf course with a Brigadier from 'Q'.

I often have to tarry on the back seat of a gharry,
It's part of my profession as a spy,
While his mind's on copulation I'm exacting information
From a senior GSO from GSI.

When I yield to the caresses of the DDWS's
I get from them the low-down on the works,
And when sleeping in the raw with a major from G4
I learn of Britain's bargain with the Turks.

On the point of the emission, in the 23rd position,
While he quavered with exotic ecstacy,
I heard of the location of a very secret station
From an over-sexed SO from OS3.

So the Colonels and the Majors, and the whisky-soaked old stagers
Enjoy themselves away from England's shore,
Why bring victory nearer when the lovelies of Gezira
Provide them with a lovely fucking war?

Base Wallopers

Australians called their staff 'Base Wallopers'.

At the end of 1942 Ali Baba, as General Morshead was then universally known, decreed that all Australians who had participated in the defence of Tobruk and its relief should wear flashes emblazoned with the letter 'T'.

Jim Sweeney, serving on the *A.I.F. News* in Cairo, composed this song for the headquarters staff lunch at 52 Kasr-el-Nil, Cairo, Christmas, 1942.

Be not dismayed, Base Wallopers,
No humble pie are we;
'Tis not decreed that we shall flaunt,
Our colours shaped in 'T'.

Beira, Birka, bints – all that,
From bar to bar we flee,
Ye heads on high,
Oh! hear our cry,
Please shape our colours 'B'.

Horseferry Road

Later in the war, after D-Day, Australians fighting in Europe revised and adapted a song their fathers had sung in similar circumstances in World War I. The original was not quite so rude.

To the tune of 'The Mountains of Mourne'

He was stranded alone in London and strode
To army headquarters in Horseferry Road,
And there met a poofter lance-corporal who said:
'You've got blood on your tunic and mud on your head.
You look so disgraceful that people will laugh,'
Said the cold-footed bastard from Horseferry staff.

The Digger jumped up with a murderous glance,
Said: 'Fuck you! I just came from the trenches in France,
Where fighting was plenty and cunt was for few,
And brave men were dying for shit-bags like you.

'You speak to a soldier you meet in the street,
And tell him you suffer with trench-bitten feet,
While you stopped back in London and missed all the strafe,
You greasy big bastard from Horseferry staff.'

The matter soon got to the ears of Lord Gort,
Who gave the whole matter a good deal of thought.
He shouted the Digger some beer in a glass,
And gave the lance-corporal a boot up the arse.

The Twats In The Ops Room

RAF bomber crews had problems of their own.

To the tune of 'John Brown's Body'

We had been flying all day long at one hundred fucking feet,
The weather fucking awful, fucking rain and fucking sleet,
The compass it was swinging fucking south and fucking north,
But we made a fucking landfall in the Firth of Fucking Forth.

CHORUS
Ain't the Air Force fucking awful?
Ain't the Air Force fucking awful?
Ain't the Air Force fucking awful?
We made a fucking landing in the Firth of Fucking Forth.

We joined the Air Force 'cos we thought it fucking right,
But don't care if we fucking fly or fucking fight,
But what we do object to are those fucking Ops Room twats,
Who sit there sewing stripes on at the rate of fucking knots.

9

A Soldier Came on Leave One Day

THE SECOND FRONT SONG
*'My little Nell was lying there exposing all her charms
. . . in a Yankee MP's arms.'*

One of the fears that torment men away fighting a war is that their wives and girl-friends back home are being unfaithful to them. In World War II these fears were sometimes justified.

The mood of the men in the 'theatres of war' was hardly improved by the arrival of large numbers of American and other foreign servicemen in their home countries – highly-paid compared with themselves, and laden with luxuries almost unheard of in wartime: liquor, silk stockings, chewing gum, tinned fruit salad.

Not unnaturally, it was asked by 'Our Boys' why they couldn't swap places with the Yanks, and go home and defend their own countries while the latter took their turn at the front.

Rumours abounded that the Yanks were stealing soldiers' wives, and even that some of the women (receiving too little money from their disgracefully underpaid husbands) had started brothels for them. Almost every soldier in North Africa had 'heard' of another who came home unexpectedly, to find that his wife had become a madame, and that his five children had been forced to live in the kitchen, to make room for the GI clients. It probably wasn't true; but it was believed.

The first song in this section, *White Lilies*, is a very old one. But most who know it today heard it for the first time while they were away at the war; it made many of them cry.

White Lilies

A soldier came on leave one day, one day,
And found his house without a wife.
He went upstairs to make his bed,
Until a thought came to his head.

He went into his daughter's room, her room,
And found her hanging from a beam.
He took his knife and cut her down,
And on her breast these words he found.

'Oh, Lord, I wish my child was born, was born,
And all my troubles they would end,
So dig my grave and dig it deep,
And lay white lilies at my feet.'

Now all you maidens bear in mind, in mind,
That a soldier's love is hard to find,
But if you find one good and true,
Never change that old love for a new.

The Yanks Back Home

Way out in the Western Desert, sharing holes with flies and fleas,
Sweats a mob of cursing Diggers, known as Ali Baba's Thieves.

When they left their land, Australia, for Egypt's foreign shores,
They were met with cries of 'Diggah! Fight like hell for freedom's cause.'

Those at home, as information of their doings filtered through,
Basked in their reflected glory – 'Look what ANZAC's sons can do!'

Now as Nippon's sons came nearer, Yankee doughboys filled their land,
And the people quickly forgetting, worship troops from foreign lands.

'We must entertain these soldiers from this mighty dollar land.
'We must give them brighter Sundays, we must give them hot-dog stands.

'They are here where danger mocks us, not in Egypt's foreign clime,
'They are here and they'll protect us. Let us give them a good time.'

So the Digger in the desert reads his three-months'-old *Melbourne Sun*,
Where it states the Yanks considered his cities are graveyards and have no fun.

Reads McArthur, their homeland's kingpin threatens Japs with merry hell,
And the people are rejoicing: 'Dougie threatens! All is well.'

Leagues away the Ninth Division, also known as Tobruk Rats,
Move once more to desert stations, once more fronting Deutschland's cracks.

Not for them those brighter Sundays, not for them those victory molls.
Only Spandau's deadly laughter and the Stuka's screaming hell.

Then to hell with those who ditched us, and o'er many a rationed bar,
We shall tell how we toured Egypt, while the Yankies fought the war.

The Second Front Song

Now my boys if you will listen, I'll sing you a little song
So sit you down a while here, I won't detain you long.
I was serving in the infantry, was told I would receive
With all the other blokes a weekend's embarkation leave.

CHORUS:
It's here, chums, it's here, chums, it's the Second Front for you.
In spite of the old Atlantic Wall we're the boys to see it through.
It won't take long to finish it, when we have got their range.
And then we can all go home and live like humans for a change.

So I packed my bag at the double, and I was ready soon.
I took my place in an army truck with the rest of my platoon.
Nobody made much noise that trip, the driver he drove blind,
We were all too busy thinking of the ones we'd leave behind.

CHORUS:
It's here chums, *etc.*

When we reached the railway station, the queue was three miles long.
They'd have filled the Wembley Stadium and still left quite a throng.
'So it's every man for himself, lads,' cried Corporal McShane,
So we rushed that crowd with a roar, and tore our way into the train.

CHORUS:
It's here, chums *etc.*

We were all packed into the corridor, it was eighty in the shade.
The seats had all been taken by the chewing gum brigade.
They smoked their Camel cigarettes and petted with their janes,
And looked at us like we were something crept out of the drains.

CHORUS:
It's here, chums, *etc.*

For eleven long hours we stood there and watched the fields go by.
We were packed so close we couldn't even smoke and that's no lie.
And all the time the Yanks talked big and boasted they were tops,
And wrestled with their judies now and then between the stops.

CHORUS:
It's here, chums, *etc.*

At last the train reached Manchester, the station was Exchange.
It was too late to get a car or bus to Whalley Range.
I tried to flag a taxi, but I didn't stand a chance:
They'd all been commandeered to take the Yanks home from a dance.

CHORUS:
It's here, chums, *etc.*

I humped my pack upon my back and made to cross the street
And just escaped a sudden death from a madly-driven jeep.
But the thought of Nellie waiting there made happiness arise
And my heart was beating pleasantly at the thought of her surprise.

CHORUS:
It's here, chums, *etc.*

I let myself in quietly and tiptoed up the stairs.
The thought of being home again had banished all my cares.
In the bedroom then I murmured, 'Nell, your soldier boy has come,'
When a voice replied in sharp surprise: 'Say, Nell, who is this bum?'

CHORUS:
It's here, chums, *etc.*

For a moment I stood speechless and rooted to the ground,
And then I switched the light on, and what d'yer think I found?
My little Nell was lying there exposing all her charms
Like the famous Whore of Babylon, in a Yankee MP's arms.

CHORUS:
It's here, chums, *etc.*

This geezer looked me over and then sat bolt upright.
He was wearing my pyjamas – the ones with purple stripes.
He made a sudden movement and tried to grab his gun
When I landed him a good straight left and stopped his bleeding fun.

CHORUS:
It's here, chums, *etc.*

And then I waded in my boys, and pasted him like hell
That bastard lost so many teeth he couldn't even yell.
I kicked him down the stairs, my lads, and out into the street.
That geezer must have thought it was the middle of next week.

CHORUS:
It's here, chums, *etc.*

My story's nearly over, there's little left to tell.
I wasn't wearing any overtures from that little Nell.
And every time I think of her, with grief my body fills.
But she'll do all right so long as there's a Yank to pay the bills.

Ewan McColl

My Faithless English Rose

To the tune of 'Lili Marlene'

I've just returned to England from somewhere overseas,
Instead of love and kisses, the girls gave me the breeze;
Said they preferred the Yanks and gum,
A little jeep, a country run,
My good-time English sweetheart,
My faithless English Rose.

I've been away a long time with thoughts of coming home,
My heart was full of gladness, and love I'd never known,
But during my absence long and grim,
The Yanks had bought, with lime and gin
My good-time English sweetheart,
My faithless English Rose.

I've been and asked the Army to put me on a ship,
Folks will think I'm barmy to do another trip,
But when my life blood begins to flow
My thoughts will flow to Yanks at home,
My faithless English sweetheart,
My faithless English Rose.

Our Country

Far across the ocean lies a land so fair and sweet,
Rugged hills and valleys, with their houses small and neat,
Once a land so free and easy, home of England's fighting sons,
Now a home of Poles and Frenchmen, Yanks and some Canadians.

In the towns and in the country, where we used to walk,
You can hear them boast and swagger, using bragging talk:
What they'll do when they get started, how they'll finish off the war,
What they're going to do to Jerry – but we've heard it all before.

In the meantime in the desert, far from sweethearts, far from wives,
Britons tough and hardened, fighting like madmen for their lives,
Tired and thirsty, scorched and blistered, blinded by the sun and sand,
Half-forgotten by their people in this God-forsaken land.

See him waiting every morning, for the highly-treasured mail,
Knowing what he'll find in it – once again the same old tale.
Oh, how often have I seen it, watched the agonising face,
Something in that letter tells him of the one that's in his place.

Can we curse these rank outsiders? Can we give them all the blame?
Or should these impatient women hang down their heads in shame?
In a way I'm not blaming anyone, but those few unfaithful ones.
In a way, they're worse than Jerry, do more harm to us than guns.

Remember this you wives and lovers, when you find you cannot wait:
What has your man got to live for, after he has lost his mate?
After all, you have your country, all the world's most precious land.
But without you *or* his country, all *he* has is burning sand.

In The Moonlight

I love you in your negligee,
I love you in your nightie,
But when moonlight flits across your tits,
By Christ all fucking mighty.

White Feather

I was walking down the street the other day,
When I chanced to hear a certain lady say:
'Why isn't he in khaki, or a suit of navy blue,
Fighting for his country, like other fellows do?'

I turned around, and this is what I said:
'Now, lady, look, I've only got one leg.
On two legs I'd be firmer,
But the other one's out in Burma.'

HMS Hood

HMS *Hood* was sunk in the great sea battle against the *Bismarck*, the pride of the German fleet, in May 1942. Only three out of 1,400 men survived.

A sailor sang this song to his two sisters when he was home on leave. It made them cry, and one of them, at least, still remembers the words.

To the tune of 'Holy Night'

When HMS *Hood* went down in the deep,
That was the news that made mothers weep.
For the sons who had fought for a country so proud,
Were down there below with the sea as their shroud.
They sleep in heavenly peace. Sleeping in heavenly peace.

Then came *George V*, the *Prince of Wales* too,
They took a hand in what the *Hood* had to do.
The *Suffolk*, the *Norfolk*, the *Cossack* as well,
Along with the *Rodney* shelled *Bismarck* to hell.
They sank that ship – oh, we're glad. But for our lads, we feel sad.

So mothers and wives and sweethearts be proud,
Though your dear lads have the sea as their shroud,
They were fighting for freedom, let's never forget,
The freedom they fought for will be won yet.
They sleep in heavenly peace. Sleeping in heavenly peace.

10

Wearing Khaki Bloomers

ROB 'EM ALL
'We're free with hot water but tight with the tea.'

A WAAF In A Uniform

To the tune of 'A Bird in a Gilded Cage'

I'm only a girl in uniform,
A pitiful sight to see.
Some say I'm happy and free from care.
It's not what it seems to me.
It's hard when you think
Of your wasted life,
Just stuck in a uniform.
Your beauty was sold
For your country's gold,
A WAAF in a uniform.

Khaki Issue

To the tune of 'She'll Be Coming Round the Mountain'

She'll be wearing khaki issue when she comes,
She'll be wearing khaki issue when she comes.
She'll be wearing khaki issue,
Wearing khaki issue,
Wearing khaki issue when she comes.

The Song Of The ATS

To the tune of 'She'll Be Coming Round the Mountain'

If you want to go to heaven when you die,
You must wear a khaki bonnet with a tie,
You must wear a khaki bonnet,
With ATS upon it,
If you want to go to heaven when you die.

Singing I will if you will so will I,
Singing I will if you will so will I,
Singing I will if you will,
I will if you will,
I will if you will so will I.

Working The Sperries

Miss A. Robertson writes: 'In the ATS on an ack-ack gun site during the war, we had our own particular little song. It seems a bit corny now.

'A Sperry was the name of a predictor which computed the height and speed of an enemy plane and directed the gun to fire at its future position.'

To the tune of 'Ferryboat Serenade'

When the barrage opens out to greet the raiding Huns,
Don't forget the girls out there, the girls behind the guns,
When you hear the boom of fire, and see the sky alight,
Remember they're on duty in the front line of the fight.
When the barrage has subsided, and the raiders past,
When the 'All Clear' sounds, and you get to bed at last,
More than grateful you should feel for all that they have done,
So don't forget the girls behind the guns.

CHORUS
I love to work a Sperry,
While bringing down a Jerry.
There's a noise just like a concertina,
When the Number One reports, 'I've seen her.'
All set, the guns are ready,
I shout 'Predictor steady.'
When the order 'Fire!' goes,
The shell goes up and through the nose.
One down, is that a Dornier?
Two down, I'd better warn yer,
Three down, that's the Sperry girls' serenade.

Rob 'Em All

This song was believed to have been written in the NAAFI accounts department in Ismailia, on the Suez Canal, for the girls behind the counter to sing.

To the tune of 'Bless 'Em All'

We are the NAAFI girls, warriors all,
The RASC/EFI,
Heavily laden with ill-gotten gains,
We came here to do not to die.
Once we were honest, but those days are gone,
The NAAFI has been our downfall,
We'll get no promotion this side of the ocean,
Let's make what we can – rob 'em all.

CHORUS
Rob 'em all, rob 'em all,
The long and the short and the tall,
Rob every sergeant and WO1,
Rob every corporal, show favour to none,
Oh, we'll rob every private in call,
We'd even rob General de Gaulle,
Our graft's systematic and quite democratic,
Show favour to none, rob 'em all.

We came out to Egypt to sell cups of tea,
To charge half an acker's a shame,
There's some like it strong and there's some like it weak,
But they all get it served up the same.
We're free with hot water but tight with the tea,
The mixture's too feeble to crawl,
We always rake off it, at least half the profit,
Show favour to none, rob 'em all.

CHORUS

Our rissoles are famous from Cairo to Cape,
We serve them from morning to night,
We serve them to servicemen serving abroad,
If they eat them it just serves them right,
We serve them with vigour, we serve them with Vim,
We serve them with might and with main;
Then we scrape up the drips of the rissoles and chips,
And we hash 'em and serve 'em again.

CHORUS

The Song Of The HMAS Centaur

The *Centaur* was an Australian hospital ship. In 1943, soon after this song was written, it was sunk by Japanese submarines between Port Moresby in New Guinea and Townsville, North Queensland.

To the tune of 'The Marines' Hymn'

From the shores of Sydney Harbour,
And from Melbourne bright and gay,
There embarked twelve army sisters,
On a cattle ship one day.

You'll have heard of her proportions –
She's the smallest ever seen,
And she glories in the title
Of the Midget Submarine.

She is manned by gallant seamen.
You would find to your surprise,
From the mast to the deck hand,
That they all have navy eyes.

As she tosses through the briny,
There's a flash – red, white and green,
And you're lucky if you glimpse her,
Our Midget Submarine.

'Welcome all!' declared the colonel,
'She's a tidy little craft.
But the only wash you'll see at sea
Is the white one, following aft.

'Yet you'll find she'll answer every call,
She'll always be on the scene,
And the Nips will watch with envy deep,
This Midget Submarine.'

11

The Paras

AND HE AIN'T GOING TO JUMP NO MORE
'The medicos they clapped their hands and rolled their sleeves and smiled.'

These songs, laden with gory humour about the dangers of parachuting, were regularly sung by the paratroopers before they jumped.

It wasn't that they weren't worried what happened to them – quite the opposite. They were thoroughly scared for the most part. In the words of ex-paratrooper John Petts, who contributed two of them, 'many of these songs were an attempt to overcome fear by naming it in capital letters'.

Among the authors of these songs were Major J. N. Taylor, MC, Major N. Stenning, Lieut J. C. Reidy, Cpl A. E. Wilmott and Pte R. M. King.

A 'Roman candle' or 'candle' is a parachute that has not been properly packed, and so fails to fill up with air, thus killing the man who jumps harnessed to it.

Jumping Through The Hole

To the tune of 'Knees Up, Mother Brown'

Jumping through the hole,
Jumping through the hole,
You've got to keep your trousers clean
When jumping through the hole.

Now if you get a candle,
Don't scream or make a sound;
Just cross your legs and neatly drill
Your grave into the ground.

The Man On The Flying Trapeze

He jumps through the hole with the greatest of ease,
His feet are together and so are his knees.
If his chute doesn't open he'll fall like a stone,
And we'll cart him away on a spoon!

What A Way To Die

We are reckless parachutists,
At least that's what we're told,
But when action stations sounded
Then you don't feel quite so bold,
When the press is euphemistic
We're the heroes of the sky,
But we feel deep down inside us
'What a terrible way to die.'

Up with the floor, up with the floor –
And our poor old knees are tremblin'
Stand to the door, stand to the door –
And we're seeing scores of gremlins!
Red light on – green light on
Out through the hole we go,
Gasping for breath, battered half to death
Drifting down to earth below.

Now there's some who jump to glory,
And there's some who jump to fame,
If your parachute don't open –
You'll get there just the same.
There's a big court of inquiry,
And the packer gets the sack,
But there's nothing in creation
That will ever bring you back.

Ten Little Paratroops

To the tune of 'The Ball of Kirriemuir'

Number One was first to go, he was first to jump,
His chute never opened so he didn't feel the bump.

Singing whull dae it this time. Wha' dae it noo
Yinna did it last time, canna dae it noo.

The next man to jump, he was Number Two;
He saw what happened to Number One and now he's RTU.

Singing whull, *etc.*

Number Three was next to go, he didn't bend his knee –
He fractured both his thighs and he's Category E.

Singing whull, *etc.*

The next man to go, he was Number Four,
He didn't hook up his static line before he left the door.

Singing whull, *etc.*

After him the next man, he was Number Five,
His parachute opened so he reached the ground alive.

Singing whull, *etc.*

Number Six was next to go, he didn't do so well;
He fell out of his harness and he went right down to hell.

Singing whull, *etc.*

The next man to go, he was Number Seven;
He came down on his head and he went right up to heaven.

Singing whull, *etc.*

The next man to go, he was Number Eight;
His parachute developed, but opened much too late.

Singing whull, *etc.*

The next man to go, he was Number Nine;
His legs and arms got tangled up in his rigging line.

Singing whull, *etc.*

The last man to jump, he was Number Ten;
He had a Roman candle so he'll never jump again.

Singing whull, *etc.*

You Don't Have To Push Me, I'll Go

To the tune of 'You Don't Have To Tell Me, I Know'

You don't have to push me, I'll go,
The wave of your hand tells me so,
Though I feel in my heart,
That my lines may not part,
If my chute fails to open then
I'll break my heart.
But some day they'll make a mistake,
And the WAAF packer's heart it will break,
For she'll get no promotion if the chute doesn't open,
And whether I like it or no,
You don't have to push me, I'll go.

And He Ain't Going To Jump No More

To the tune of 'John Brown's Body'

'Is everybody happy?' said the Sergeant, looking up,
Our hero feebly answered 'Yea' and then they hooked him up,
He jumped into the slipstream, and he twisted twenty times,
    And he ain't going to jump no more.

CHORUS
    Glory, glory what a hell of a way to die!
            (repeat three times)
    And he ain't going to jump no more.

He counted loud, he counted long and waited for the shock,
He felt the wind . . . he felt the air . . . he felt the awful drop,
He pulled the lines, the silk came down and wrapped around his legs,
    And he ain't going to jump no more.

CHORUS

The days he lived and loved and laughed kept running through his mind,
He thought about the medicos and wondered what they'd find,
He thought about the girl back home, the one he left behind,
    And he ain't going to jump no more.

CHORUS

The lines all wrapped around his neck; the 'D' rings broke his dome . . .
The lift webs wrapped themselves in knots around each skinny bone,
The canopy became his shroud as he hurtled to the ground,
    And he ain't going to jump no more.

CHORUS

The ambulance was on the spot, the jeeps were running wild,
The medicos they clapped their hands and rolled their sleeves and smiled,
For it had been a week or so, since that a chute had failed,
    And he ain't going to jump no more.

    CHORUS

He hit the ground, the sound was 'splat', the blood went spurting high,
His pals were heard to say, 'Oh what a pretty way to die,'
They rolled him up still in his chute, and poured him from his boots,
    And he ain't going to jump no more.

    CHORUS

There was blood upon the lift webs, there was blood upon his chute,
Blood that came a-trickling from the paratrooper's boots,
And there he lay, like jelly in the welter of his gore,
    And he ain't going to jump no more.

Passing Thoughts

To the tune of 'John Brown's Body'

I'd like to find the Sergeant who forgot to hook me up,
        (Repeat three times)
For I ain't gonna jump no more.

I'd like to find the WAAF who tied a love knot in my line,
     (Repeat three times)
For I ain't gonna jump no more.

I'd like to find the pilot who forgot to throttle back,
     (Repeat three times)
For I ain't gonna jump no more.

I'd like to find the WAAF who put the blanket in my chute,
     (Repeat three times)
For I ain't gonna jump no more.

Oh they wiped me off the tarmac like a pound of strawberry jam,
     (Repeat three times)
For I ain't gonna jump no more.

Oh Come Sit By My Side If You Love Me

To the tune of 'Red River Valley'

Oh come sit by my side if you love me,
Do not hasten to bid me adieu,
But remember the poor paratrooper,
And the job he is trying to do.

When the red light goes on we are ready,
For the Sergeant to shout, 'Number one!'
Though we sit in the plane close together,
We all tumble out one by one.

When we're coming in for a landing,
Just remember the Sergeant's advice,
Keep your feet and your knees close together,
And you'll reach mother earth very nice.

When we land in one certain country,
There's a job we will do very well,
We will fire old Goering and Adolph,
And all of those buggers as well.

So stand by your class and be ready,
And remember the men of the sky,
Here's a toast to the men dead already,
And a toast for the next man to die.

Always Keep Your Trousers Clean

To the tune of 'Knees Up, Mother Brown'

When first I came to PTS,
My CO he advised
Take lots and lots of underwear
You'll need it, I surmise,
But I replied, 'By Gad, sir,
Whatever may befall,
I'll always keep my trousers clean
When jumping through the hole.'

CHORUS
Jumping through the hole,
Jumping through the hole,
I'll always keep my trousers clean,
When jumping thru' the hole.

I went into the hangar,
Instructors by my side,
And on Kilkenny's circus
Had many a glorious ride,
On these ingenious gadgets,
Said he, 'You'll learn to fall
And keep your feet together
When you're jumping through the hole.'

CHORUS

He swung me in the swings, boys,
He shot me down the chute
He showed me the high aperture,
I thought it rather cute;
Said he, 'This apparatus
Will teach you one and all
To centralise your C of G
When jumping through the hole.'

CHORUS

I saw the gorgeous statichutes
With camouflage design,
I heard the Warrant Officer
Shoot such a lovely line,
'This lovely bit of stuff, lads,'
Said he, 'Upon my soul,
Is sweeter than your sweetheart
When you're jumping through the hole.'

CHORUS

One morning very early,
Cold and damp and dark,
They took me in a so-called bus,
Out to Tatton Park,
In keeping with the weather,
I said to one and all,
'I take a dim and misty view,
Of jumping through the hole.'

CHORUS

He fitted me with parachute,
And helmet for my head,
The Sergeant looked with expert eye,
'It fits you fine,' he said,
'I'll introduce you now to "Bessie",
That is what we call the nice balloon
From which you'll soon
Be jumping through the hole.'

CHORUS

'OK, up six hundred,
Four to drop,' said he.
'Four to drop, Good God!' I cried,
'And one of them is me!'
So clinging very tightly to
The handles on the floor
I cursed the day I volunteered,
For jumping through the hole.

CHORUS

He told me a funny story,
I couldn't see the joke,
In fact, I thought he was a most
Unsympathetic bloke,
But when he shouted, 'Action stations!'
Then he shouted 'GO!'
I simply couldn't stop myself,
From jumping through the hole.

CHORUS

I hit my pack, I rang the 'bell',
I twisted twenty times
I came down with both feet entangled
In the rigging lines
But floating upside down to earth
I didn't care at all
For I had kept my trousers clean
When jumping through the hole.

CHORUS

You're So Nice To Come Down With

To the tune of 'You'd Be So Nice To Come Home To'

You're so nice to come down with,
When the aircraft's out of sight,
Up above me you look so lovely,
In your silk gown flowing white.

And it's so nice to see you,
And to know you are safe up above,
I'm your paratroop, you're my statichute,
Can't live without you, my love!

The Merry Month Of May

To the tune of 'Far, Far Away'

On her leg she wears a silken garter,
She wears it in the springtime, in the merry month of May,
And if you ask her why the hell she wears it,
She wears it for her paratrooper,
Far, far away.

       Far away, far away,
       She wears it for her paratrooper,
       Far, far away.

Around the park she wheels a perambulator,
She wheels it in the springtime, in the merry month of May,
And if you ask her why the hell she wheels it,
She wheels it for her paratrooper,
Far, far away.

       Far away, far away, *etc.*

Behind the door her father keeps a shotgun,
He keeps it in the springtime, in the merry month of May,
And if you ask him why the hell he keeps it
He keeps it for that paratrooper,
Far, far away.

       Far away, far away, *etc.*

The paratrooper went to join his unit,
He joined it in the springtime, in the merry month of May,
And if you ask him why the hell he joined it,
He joined it to be very, very,
Far, far away.

       Far away, far away, *etc.*

In her hand she holds a bunch of daisies,
She holds them in the springtime, in the merry month of May,
And if you ask her why the hell she holds them,
She holds them for a paratrooper,
. . . six feet down.

    Six feet down,
    Six feet down,
    She holds them for a paratrooper
    Six feet down.

12

Flying

A25 SONG
'...In the Fleet Air Arm the prospects are grim
If the landing's piss-poor and the pilot can't swim.'

Laying Eggs In The Sky

To the tune of 'My Bonnie Lies Over the Ocean'

We're making a beeline for Berlin,
Blindfolded, we'll soon find the way.
We're making a beeline for Berlin,
Though no one will ask us to stay.
It's true that we've not been invited –
We just want to spring a surprise.
We bet poor old Fritz
Will have forty-nine fits
When we start laying eggs in the sky,
When we start laying eggs in the sky.

It's Foolish, But It's Fun

To the tune of 'It's Foolish, But It's Fun'

I love to be a WOP/AG,
And fly all over Germanee,
And get shot up to buggeree,
It's foolish, but it's fun.

Who'll Fly A Wimpey?

To the tune of 'Waltzing Matilda'

Who'll fly a Wimpey, who'll fly a Wimpey,
Who'll fly a Wimpey over Germanee?
I, said the pilot, I, said the pilot,
I'll fly a Hercules Mark Three.

I'll set the course, sir, I'll set the course, sir,
I'll set the course on my little CSC,
And if you keep to the course that I have set, sir,
Then we will fly over Germanee.

I'll shoot 'em down, sir, I'll shoot 'em down, sir,
I'll shoot 'em down if they don't shoot at me.
Then we'll go to the Ops Room and shoot a fucking line, sir,
And then we'll all get the DFC.

I'll press the tit, sir, I'll press the tit, sir,
I'll press the tit at the first flak we see,
'Cos I don't like the flak, sir, I don't like the flak, sir,
I want nothing but plenty of height for me.

How is the Met, sir, how is the Met, sir,
How is the Met? – it looks very dud to me.
Let's scrub it out, sir, let's scrub it out, sir,
'Cos I've got a date fixed with my popsie.

Flying By Night And By Day

We're leaving Khartoum by the light of the moon,
We're flying by night and by day.
We're out in the heat and we've fuck all to eat,
'Cos we've thrown all our rations away.

Flying Flying Fortresses

Rick Yeldap writes: 'This was preferably sung in American Air Force preserves, with the resultant punch-up.'

To the tune of 'John Brown's Body'

Flying flying fortresses at forty thousand feet,
Flying flying fortresses at forty thousand feet,
Flying flying fortresses at forty thousand feet,
We've got bags of ammunition and a teeny weeny bomb,
As we go rolling on.

But fly Avro Lancasters at zero zero feet,
Flying Avro Lancasters at zero zero feet,
Flying Avro Lancasters at zero zero feet,
We've got fuck-all ammunition, and a great big blooming bomb,
As we go rolling on.

A25 Song

Rupert Burrowe writes: 'During World War II the Fleet Air Arm was known as the Air Branch of the Royal Navy. Naval fliers during the war referred to their service as "The Branch", carefully distinguishing themselves from other naval personnel whom they grouped together under the sobriquet "Fish-heads".

'Because of the nature of naval aviation, the accident rate was rather high (in one operation involving experienced crews, of 101 aircraft written off, 39 were lost in combat and the remainder in deck landings and other accidents).

'Accidents were unfortunate enough in themselves, but to the survivors of these was added the burden of filling in an accident report form (Form A25), so detailed and so lengthy as to suggest that death by drowning was a desirable alternative. By custom, the report had to begin with the words "I have the honour to report . . ." – which always seemed rather inappropriate when they were followed by something like, ". . . that I missed the arrestor wires and crashed into three parked aircraft, destroying them all."

'The following further explanatory notes to this song are unfortunately necessary. When deck-landing, the pilot followed the signals of the "batsman" ("Bats") who indicated whether he should go higher, lower, slower, etc. . . . On touchdown, the hook of the aircraft, lowered from the cockpit, was supposed

to catch one of the carrier's arrestor wires which ran transversely across the deck.

'If this failed to engage, a more serious accident was avoided by collison with a wire barrier which was raised across the deck, abreast the after-end of the superstructure. The latter had a small platform at its after-end which was an ideal spot from which to watch aircraft landing. Known as the "Goofer's Gallery", "Wings" was usually there.'

To the tune of 'If Moonlight Don't Kill Me, I'll Live Till I Die'

They say in the Air Force a landing's OK,
If the pilot gets out and can still walk away.
But in the Fleet Air Arm the prospects are grim
If the landing's piss-poor and the pilot can't swim.

> Cracking show, I'm alive,
> But I've still got to render my A25!

They gave me a Seafire to beat up the fleet,
I beat up the *Nelson* and *Rodney* a treat,
But forgot the high mast that sticks out from *Formid*.
And a seat in the Goofers was worth fifty quid.

> Cracking show, *etc.*

I thought I was coming in low enough but
I was twenty feet up when the batsman gave 'cut!'
And loud in my earholes the sweet angels sang,
'Float . . . float . . . float . . . float . . . float . . . float barrier – Prang!'

> Cracking show, *etc.*

When the batsman made 'lower' I always went higher,
Bounced on the deck and missed the last wire,
A bloody great barrier loomed up in front,
And Wings shouted 'Switch off your engine, you CUNT!'

> Cracking show, *etc.*

13

In the
Prison Camps

WAITING FOR SOMETHING TO HAPPEN
'We'd all be happier, feel a lot snappier,
If something would happen again.'

Well over 200,000 British, ANZAC, Canadian and other Empire forces were captured and made prisoners during the war. 'Sods' Operas' were regularly held in most of the camps – even in Japanese ones, where the conditions were so terrible, they somehow found the energy to put them on from time to time.

Many of the songs in this section come from the concert parties Slim de Grey and Ray Tullipan (the first a professional singer and the second an amateur dance- and brass-band performer, both of whom enlisted with the Australian Imperial Force) organised at the notorious Changi Prison Camp, Singapore.

Brigadier F. G. Galleghan, who was commander of Australian prisoners of war in Singapore, writes: 'In the early days, the members of the Concert Party moved from area to area carrying their properties and using an old rickshaw that had found its way to camp. It was from this sight that the idea of using an existing building as a theatre was conceived. And what set-backs ensued!

'A theatre was built and almost completed by the members of the concert party themselves, when the grim Barrack Square Incident took place and later, in the usual Japanese fashion, the use of the building was withdrawn. Not daunted, the concert party built another theatre, which served all the prisoners of war from early 1943 to early 1944 . . .

'I couple the work of the A.I.F. Concert Party with that of the Australian Army Medical Corps. One performed yeoman service to keep men physically fit, and the other kept men fit mentally.'

Waiting For Something To Happen

Waiting for something to happen
Turns all our laughter to tears,
There's no use a-worrying, no use a-hurrying,
We may be waiting for years.

Waiting for someone to take us,
We can't go home on a tram,
Maybe Americans, maybe the Chinamen,
Maybe the Japs'll say scram.

We've had malaria and beri-beri,
But now we've caught
A nasty rash that makes it very very
Hard for us to walk.

Waiting for something to happen,
Might even drive you insane.
We'd all be happier, feel a lot snappier,
If something would happen again.

All Dressed Up

All dressed up and nowhere to go,
Never a chance to dance, never a show,
Sentimental kind of people like me
Just keep on dreaming,
You know how unhappy dreamers can be.
All alone with no one to love,
Patiently wishing on stars up above,
Until someone comes along I'll always be blue
I know,
All dressed up and nowhere to go.

Just A Bungalow Called Home

There's a charming place I see in all my dreams,
It's serene and peaceful and how real it seems,
It's a place I know,
Just a bungalow,
Called home.

Sunbeams sparkle gaily on the morning dew,
Breezes whisper softly through the trees I knew,
Bidding me to go
To a bungalow,
Called home.

See the folks are sitting on the lawn,
Just in the shade of the old honeysuckle tree,
And as the sun is sinking in the west,
They send a message saying that they'll always think of me.

Perfumes from the daffodil and roses rare,
Form a scented bouquet on the evening air,
In the after-glow,
Round a bungalow,
Called home.

Feelin' Tired

Feelin' tired, lazy as can be,
Feelin' tired 'neath a shady tree,
Sleepy old stream just goes eddying by,
Murmuring a dreamy lullaby.

Not a care, nothing on my mind,
Ev'rywhere peacefulness I find,
Drowsy old stream slowly swirling along,
Croons to me a melancholy song.

Tired, just can't help lazin',
Amazin' how dreary I feel,
Tired, just can't help dozin',
Supposin' my dreams are real.

Feelin' tired, lazin' all the day,
Yawnin' wide, sleepin' time away.
Dozin' and dreamin' I feel satisfied,
'Cause I'm everlastin' feelin' tired.

Looking At The Moon

Looking at the moon, Mmmmm,
Humming on a tune, Mmmmm,
Wondering if you are looking at the moon tonight.
Picturing your charms, Mmmmm,
Need you in my arms, Mmmmm,
If you were with me I'm sure that everything would be just right.
I'm so alone 'neath a starry sky,
All on my own and I wonder why,
I'm looking at the moon, Mmmmm,
Hoping very soon, Mmmmm,
You and I will be together looking at the moon.

Keep Smiling

Keep smiling, don't be blue dear,
My thoughts are all of you dear,
I would feel so low
If I thought that you were shedding tears, so,
Keep smiling, don't you cry dear,
Or you'll have me crying too,
We're like birds of a feather,
Very soon we'll be together, so
Keep smiling, keep me smiling too.

Keep Singing

If you sing a song the whole day long,
You'll find that things just can't go wrong,
And everyone will have a smile for you.

Any old tune you know,
Fast, slow or hot or sweet and low,
Just keep on singing, that's the thing to do.

With a smiling face just set the pace,
Then Old Man Gloom's not in the race
And you will have no time for feeling blue.

So raise a smile, sing all the while
And take a rosey view.
Just keep on singing, that's the thing to do.

When We Sail Down The River

Mr J. Burns writes: 'At POW Camp Borneo, where I was one of the residents, we had a concert party weekly, and I was the singer. The most popular song was the one that we all sang with gusto at the end of the show':

When we sail down the river to the sea,
When this jail becomes another memory,
We'll be free, as we were in days of yore,
And we'll see life as we never saw before.
Let the Dyaks, and the Dutchmen, and the Chinese
fight about it,
They can keep their Borneo, 'cos we can
do without it,
When we sail down the river to the sea,
There'll be happy happy days, for you and me.

Swing Song

Written in Mooselargl Prison Camp, 1943.

Now, my little lad
   Is the image of his dad.
He is his mother's pride and joy.
   I take him upstairs
To watch him say his prayers,
   'Please God, make me a good little boy.'
I tuck him in and sing him
   Songs my mother used to sing.
He looks at me and says
   He does not like that kind of swing,
'So sing me to sleep with a swing song,
   And I'll be a good little boy.
I know you're not Bing,
   But you must give me swing,
It's the only kind of rhythm I enjoy.
   You give me grey hairs
With your three little bears,
   And you silly little pigs that went to market.
I don't give a yen
   For your ten nigger men,
So sing me to sleep with a swing song.'

14

Invasion!

THE D-DAY DODGERS
'We landed at Salerno, a holiday with pay.
Jerry brought his bands out to cheer us on our way.'

On 3 September 1943 – the fourth anniversary of the declaration of war – the 8th Army crossed the Mediterranean and landed with a thump on Italy's big toe. The main attack was launched on Salerno six days later. Although the Italians had secretly surrendered by then, the German forces in Italy fought back fiercely. There had been no chance of surprising them and our casualties were heavy. But we had a foothold in Europe again.

The Allies' progress northward was contested all the way. Cassino was not taken until the next year after a long and terrible battle. The landings at Anzio and the fall of Rome followed a month later. It took a year to break through the Gothic Line and capture Bologna.

By this time, the troops were exhausted and not a little fed up. In particular, they suspected people back home, and politicians especially, of indifference and ingratitude, symbolised – in their eyes – by the Government's failure to so much as lay on even the smallest supply of beer for them.

Thousands of soldiers in Italy vented their feelings by singing the *D-Day Dodgers* song. How accurately it expressed their anger is shown by the fact that as a result of my appeals for contributions for this book, I received no less than twenty-three copies of it, from many different parts of Britain.

The term 'D-Day Dodgers' is attributed to Nancy, Lady Astor, Britain's first woman MP and a harsh-spoken, American-born, Tory matron who campaigned tirelessly against sex and drink.

In October 1944 Lady Astor was a member of an all-party Parliamentary delegation that was allowed to visit Italy to study the troops' living conditions. It is said that as a result, she not merely described the troops as 'D-Day Dodgers', but declared them to be drunken and dissolute. She was also said to have opined that as so many had spent so much of their time in brothels, the incidence of VD among them was extremely high; and that when they came home on leave, they should be made to wear yellow arm-bands, so that British womanhood could identify them for what they were, and be warned.

Lady Astor herself indignantly and repeatedly denied that she had ever thought, let alone uttered, anything of the kind. She wrote to the editor of the *Daily Mirror*, asking him to publish her denial, but received a somewhat brusque refusal.

Recent searches through newspapers of the period, Hansard's reports of Parliamentary debates and Lady Astor's own papers have failed to bring to light any record of her remarks, if in fact she did make them.

What is beyond question is that virtually every British serviceman in Italy was convinced that she did, and regarded her alleged remarks as typical of the slurs being made against them back home. The accepted version is that she made the remarks in the House of Commons, and that Winston Churchill only disowned her when the protests from the front became intense.

For the 8th Army and the rest, one of the greatest sources of discontent was that their colleagues fighting in France (who had landed on D-Day) were already getting home leave, whereas they themselves had fought their way through North Africa and Italy for as long as two years, without any.

The D-Day Dodgers

To the tune of 'Lili Marlene'

We are the D-Day Dodgers, out in Italy,
Always on the vino, always on the spree.
Eighth Army skivers and their tanks,
We go to war in ties like swanks.
For we are the D-Day Dodgers, in sunny Italy.

We landed at Salerno, a holiday with pay.
Jerry brought his bands out to cheer us on our way,
Showed us the sights and gave us tea,
We all sang songs, the beer was free.
For we are the D-Day Dodgers, the lads that D-Day dodged.

Palermo and Cassino were taken in our stride,
We did not go to fight there, we just went for the ride.
Anzio and Sangro are just names,
We only went to look for dames,
For we are the D-Day Dodgers, in sunny Italy.

On our way to Florence, we had a lovely time,
We drove a bus from Rimini, right through the Gothic Line,
Then to Bologna we did go,
And went bathing in the Po,
For we are the D-Day Dodgers, the lads that D-Day dodged.

We hear the boys in France are going home on leave,
After six months' service, such a shame they're not relieved.
And we're told to carry on a few more years,
Because our wives don't shed no tears.
For we are the D-Day Dodgers, out in sunny Italy.

Once we had a 'blue light' that we were going home,
Back to dear old Blighty, never more to roam.
Then someone whispered: 'In France we'll fight,'
We said: 'Not that, we'll just sit tight,'
For we are the D-Day Dodgers, the lads that D-Day dodged.

Dear Lady Astor, you think you know a lot,
Standing on a platform and talking tommy rot.
Dear England's sweetheart and her pride,
We think your mouth is much too wide –
From the D-Day Dodgers, out in sunny Italy.

Look around the hillsides, through the mist and rain,
See the scattered crosses, some that bear no name.
Heartbreak and toil and suffering gone,
The lads beneath, they slumber on.
They are the D-Day Dodgers who'll stay in Italy.

Lucky Fellers

Before dawn on D-Day – 6 June 1944 – advance parties of paratroopers were landed behind the German lines in gliders, with the task of creating panic and alarm among the enemy as the Normandy beaches were stormed.

To the tune of 'Bless 'Em All'

Thousands of gliders were leaving their base,
Bound for a foreign shore,
Heavily laden with my pals and me,
Going by air 'cos we daren't go by sea.
So we're saying goodbye to them all,
As into our gliders we crawl.
We are lucky fellers – we've got no propellers.
So cheer up, my lads, bless 'em all.

The Legion Of The Lost

This sombre marching song was composed, appropriately enough, by a church organist, serving with the King's Regiment, Liverpool.

Legion of the Lost they call us,
The Legion of the Lost are we
Legion arms before us
Marching on to victory
Marching on to hell with the flag flying
Marching on to hell with the band playing
Can't you hear the beat of the drum saying:
Scum, scum, with every tap of the drum,
Saying scum of the earth
Scum of the earth still they come
To fight and die for victory
The Legion of the Lost are we.

Men Of Hardwick

To the tune of 'Men of Harlech'

Men of Hardwick never grumble
As their Whitley engines rumble,
Through the hole they gladly tumble,
Ready for the fray.

Laughing as they're downward sweeping,
While the Jerries all are sleeping;
Many frauleins will be weeping
At the dawn of day.

Battle drums are beating
While the foe is fleeting.
Many Huns will gladly run
And all in disorder retreating.

Downwards, downwards on to glory,
Many the man will tell his story,
Of the deeds both dark and gory,
Gallant Hardwick Men.

The Rooty Song

This World War I song was sung again by soldiers in France in 1944.

At times we get some rooty,
You civvies call it bread.
It ain't as light as fevers,
And it ain't exactly lead.

But we gets it down us somehow
And we never sends it back,
Though it's covered up with whiskers,
That gets rubbed off the sack.

We gets no eggs for breakfast,
They sends us over shells,
And we dives into our dugouts,
And gets laughed at by our pals.

The Irish Fusiliers

To the tune of 'Lili Marlene'

Though you're seldom told the Faughs are in the war,
Even though you've never heard the name before,
You will discover one fine day,
The Faughs have shown the rest the way,
The Irish Fusiliers. The Irish Fusiliers.

Whenever there's a battle to break the Jerry line,
You can be sure you'll see the shamrock shine,
Storming the heights or on the plains,
In summer's heat or winter's rain,
The Irish Fusiliers. The Irish Fusiliers.

You can have your tanks and all your SP guns,
They're not the chaps who really chase the Huns,
Give us the Gunners of 17th Field,
Between us both we'll make them yield,
The Irish Fusiliers. The Irish Fusiliers.

When all the others think they've done enough,
That's when you'll find the Fusiliers are tough;
78th Division soon found out
They couldn't hope to win without
The Irish Fusiliers. The Irish Fusiliers.

The Royal Artillery

To the tune of 'Back Home in Tennessee'

I enlisted as a Gunner
In the King's RA,
For four and nine a day,
Which wasn't too bad pay.
But it's all 'Jump to it,' 'Run there,'
And 'Man that gun there,'
All the lousy day.
And each evening,
In the wet canteen,
We sing this roundelay:

We are tired hands,
Too tired to even stand.
Our Sergeant Major,
He's a regular twit, you see.
And our officers too,
Are the worst I ever knew.
Talk about leaders,
They ought to be in feeders.
Oh, what shall we do?
We'll offer up our thanks,
Thank heaven we've got the tanks,
The WRAAFs and Air Force too,
And when this show is over,
I'll beat it hotfoot back to Dover
And departee, gay and hearty,
To my home in Battersea.

15

The Forgotten Armies

WAIT TILL YOU GET TO NEW GUINEA
'Then they sat us down in the jungle,
And we had a very good look
At the excellent guide for tourists
Compiled by Thomas Cook.'

The men who felt most neglected, to the point of being virtually abandoned, by the people back home, were those fighting the Japanese in Asia and the Pacific.

Their war, of course, continued for several months after the collapse of Germany.

Down By Mandalay

Out there in the jungle, down by Mandalay,
A few forgotten soldiers slowly fight their way.
They dream of the girls they left back home,
And soon they hope to cross the foam
To see their land and loved ones,
Never more to roam.

Some of them are repat, some are time expired,
Longing for their troopship, and their fireside.
They often talk of Burmese plains,
Of dust and heat and monsoon rains,
Of roads that lead to heaven,
And tracks that lead to hell.

Now all you lads from Blighty, who travel far from home,
Who never liked the cities of Tripoli and Rome,
Remember the lads who fought and dwelt
In jungles green, where brasses melt,
And Japs were more like monkeys
And mossie bites were felt.

Now when this war is over and the job is done,
All you lads from Burma go tell it to your son:
'Remember the war against the Hun,
But don't forget the war they won,
In Asia's south-east corner,
Against the Rising Sun.'

Bury Me Out In The Jungle

To the tune of 'The Eton Boating Song'

'Twas out at that place called Kohima,
Where most of the fighting was done,
'Twas there that a lad from the Borders
Fell to a Japanese gun.

Now as he lay there in the jungle
And the blood from his wounds did flow red,
He gathered his comrades around him
And these are the words that he said.

'Oh, bury me out in the jungle,
Under the old Burma sun,
Bury me out in the jungle,
My duty to England is done.'

So, they buried him out in the jungle,
By the light of the far setting sun,
They buried him out in the jungle
His job for his country was done.

Now when you get back to old Blighty
And the war is all over and won,
Just remember that poor British Tommy
Under the old Burma sun.

Now if she had only been faithful,
He might have been raising a son,
But instead he's just pushing up teak trees,
Under the old Burma sun.

South Of Meiktila

To the tune of 'South of the Border'

South of Meiktila, down Pyawbe way,
That's where the Jap thought that they had come to stay.
The Borders surprised them one sunny day.
South of Meiktila, down Pyawbe way.

Then in went 'B' Company, led by Long John,
And Major Patch MC took 'A' Company along.
'C' Company behind them, with Tommo in charge.
'D' were right forward, near the barrage.

Then the Japs started shouting and screaming,
When the mortar platoon got weaving.
But the boys didn't need any screening.
Oh! for the Japs, they were on the run.

South of Meiktila, down Pyawbe way,
That's where the CO said, 'You'll all salute to the front today.'
Fifty Div. passed through us, on to Toungoo.
Two-sixty flanked us, by taking Rangoon.

Bombay Bibley

In India, the British troops found their welcome less than effusive.

This bitter song about a Bombay tart was sung, writes L. K. Howlett, who served with the Gordon Highlanders, 'by hundreds of British who served in India. I first heard it as a very young soldier while stationed in Mkow, and later on in numerous wet canteens and on the march, from the North-West Frontier, even up into Burma.'

The words in soldiers' pidgin Hindi are inevitably mostly of obscene reference, and interested readers will be able to work out their meanings for themselves.

As I was walking down Ship Street,
For my weekly grind,
I heard a Bombay bibley bolo from behind.
'Hitherao, soldier! Pu cara me,
Cushnay pukharo kiswasti.
Aye, yai, wasan chae, Bombay bibley bught acha.'
MAY THE BOAT THAT TAKES YOU OVER
SINK TO THE BOTTOM OF THE PANI SAHIB!

'Ek pici for hubble bubble.
Doh pici for chuggaree,
Ten pici for muchi-muchi,
Master makit barbaree.
Aye, yai, wasan chae, Bombay bibley bught acha.'
MAY THE BOAT THAT TAKES YOU OVER
SINK TO THE BOTTOM OF THE PANI SAHIB!

Spud Spedding's Broken Boys

'Spud' was the nickname of Colonel Spedding of the Border Regiment, which fought and suffered considerably in the Burma campaign.

Now it appeared on orders,
That I should join the Borders,
To be one of Spud Spedding's Broken Boys.

So seeing I was willing,
They packed me off to Bilin,
To be one of Spud Spedding's Broken Boys.

Now I hadn't been there long,
When they sent me to Taungzun,
'Cos I'm one of Spud Spedding's Broken Boys.

I thought I was going home,
But they ordered us to Prome,
We're some of Spud Spedding's Broken Boys.

But they hadn't finished yet, you know,
For they sent us to Thayetmyo,
'Cos we are Spud Spedding's Broken Boys.

Poor lad, his name was Andy,
He became a Minden Dandy,
He's one of Spud Spedding's Broken Boys.

We saw the rations through,
At milestone twenty-two,
We're some of Spud Spedding's Broken Boys.

And if I'd been a farmer,
I might have gone to Kama,
Like some of Spud Spedding's Broken Boys.

And I think they got it wrong –
No guns at Shwemaungzaung?
I'm one of Spud Spedding's Broken Boys.

Yes, we caught them single-handed,
But now the mob's disbanded,
And where are Spud Spedding's Broken Boys?

Now if I'd tried rather harder,
I'd have made the UK cadre
And stayed with Spud Spedding's Broken Boys.

But I sadly packed my bedding,
And I left the ranks of Spedding,
We're no longer Spud Spedding's Broken Boys.

For the army we were hired,
But now we're time expired,
So here's to Spud Spedding's Broken Boys!

Tipperary (Burma)

To the tune of 'It's a Long Way to Tipperary'

It's a long time since I saw Blighty,
It's a long time ago,
It's a long time since I left Blighty
To fight to Tokyo.

Goodbye, Jungle Burma,
Malay, Singapore,
It's a long, long time since I saw Blighty,
But I'll soon be there.

Wait Till You Get To New Guinea

This monologue has been included despite its length, because it is one of the best of its kind to come from the war. It was written by one of the Australians who, after the victory in North Africa, went back to the Antipodes to fight the 'Nips'. But the precise identity of the author is uncertain.

We were only Alamein Pansies,
Tel-el-Eisa just a spree,
We had played golf on the Hill of Jesus,
Played marbles on old 33.

We had won the Benghazi handicap,
By the merest of flaming flukes.
The playboys of the desert,
We lived like flaming dukes.

We had only been one year before
The Rats of old Tobruk,
With beer in pails on Saturday nights,
On Sundays, wild roast duck.

We played the South Africans cricket,
Ice cream, cake, beer in pails,
Brass bands played on Saturday nights,
While we danced with Oulandi gals.

It was the same all over,
Wherever we tourists went,
Syria, Crete or Alex,
Always on pleasure bent.

Montgomery rather liked us,
The Kiwis liked us too,
They must have been good people.
They said to us, 'You'll do.'

This suited us down to the ground,
Together there could be no failure.
But the wily Jap was going so well,
That they sent us home to Australia.

So we went to Ali Baba and said,
'What about it, Les?'
He cogitated a minute or two,
And said: 'The answer is yes.'

So we sailed away from Suez,
And patted ourselves on the back.
We had won the battles of Sister Street,
The Burka and El Shat.

We liked ourselves a little bit,
Till to Aussie we get.
'Wait till you get to New Guinea.
You ain't seen nothing yet.'

These were the words that greeted us
When at last we had returned.
We blushed to the back of our necks,
And our ears began to burn.

'Where have you been, these three long years,
And Aussie in dire distress?
Now lend a hand, you Desert Rats,
And pull us out of this mess.

'You think you've done a hell of a lot,
On that we'll take a bet.
But wait till you get to New Guinea.
You ain't seen nothing yet.'

So to Ali Baba again we went,
And said, 'What about it, Les?'
We discussed the plan for a minute or so,
And said, 'Off to New Guinea we go.'

So we sailed away from Moreton Bay,
Shaken to our very core.
We shivered and shook in our desert skins,
As we sighted the dreaded shore.

Then they sat us down in the jungle,
And we had a very good look
At the excellent guide for tourists
Compiled by Thomas Cook.

And we racked our brains and argued,
'Now where will we make our stay?'
Till someone said we'd been lying a year,
'So I think it had better be Lae.'

So before we left, where we first spied the shore,
We listened to the tales they told,
Of the Nipponese tiger in every tree,
Ferocious, cunning and bold.

And we turned as learners will do,
Asked these fellows of tales where they'd been.
And much to our surprise we discovered the truth,
That many a Jap they had seen.

So armed with this knowledge,
We sailed away one day,
Off on the road to adventure,
To the romantic city of Lae.

We did not pull right into the town,
As we were rather shy.
Reception committees are not our style,
So we passed the city by.

We thought we'd try the jungle trails,
There was hardly a one, what a laugh.
So we hacked our way through the virgin bush,
Slashing from dawn to dark.

Now the powers that be, in their wisdom,
Had given us books, red and blue,
On how to live in New Guinea,
And what a jungle soldier should do.

On paper, this was all hunky dory,
But things have got to be tried.
Had we did what the good book told us,
We'd all have bloody well died.

In Tobruk, Lord Haw-Haw had told us,
The difference that he could see
Between us and a bloody circus,
Was that a lot more tents had we.

But being a circus was quite okay,
For it was carried through against Jerry,
And when the Eyeties heard our brass bands play,
They cheered and danced and made merry.

So once more we became a circus,
And we did all the things that ain't done.
We got along very much easier,
And it certainly was more fun.

We camped on the sides of rivers,
All went in for a swim or we'd bust,
While lurking Nipponese tigers
Hari-kiried themselves in disgust.

Our bivouacs were like Luna Park,
The fires, they were burning in piles,
And loud bursts of raucous laughter
Could be heard in the jungle for miles.

The Tojos were clear dumbfounded,
They did not know where to begin.
For when we contacted their tigers,
We did not start to dig in.

Their tigers turned out to be rabbits,
And we chased them from tree to tree,
The lads ho-hoed like foxhounds,
A-shooting and killing with glee.

These Nips had a lot to pay for:
Our tobacco and matches got wet,
Crossing swamps and flooded rivers,
With water right up to our necks.

At last we came to the Basu,
Four hundred yards wide, and in flood.
We crossed it all right in the bright moonlight,
But we paid in good Aussie blood.

They were there in impregnable positions,
Firing at us point-blank,
But we bridged the turbulent torrent,
And reached the opposite bank.

But a word in praise of the militia,
Of their labour the tale I must tell.
They're the white NG Angels all right,
As they toiled and sweated in hell.

178

178 KISS ME GOODNIGHT, SERGEANT MAJOR

They plugged along through the jungle,
On nearly unknown trails.
Cut by us a week before,
With their boxes and dixies and pails.

For they carried our bully beef well forward,
Nearly up to the firing line,
Yes, they've got the boong well beaten,
We've never seen anything so fine.

You can't curb these adventurous spirits,
There will be some tales to tell
Of their trips to the fighting soldiers,
Deep in the jungle hell.

And when the job is completed,
And we think that we're all set,
Then surely no one will tell us now
'YOU AIN'T SEEN NOTHING YET.'

But when we're relieved and to base we go,
The heroes, they'll tell us with scorn:
'You should have been here six months before,
You'd have wished you'd never been born.'

We don't really know what had changed the Jap,
For they are different men:
Ferocious, fanatical, cunning and bold,
They surely were tigers then.

For wherever we go, we will hear the same tales,
We're sure to get them in sheaves,
For are we not Ali Baba's men,
His twenty thousand thieves?

Some may say, the game is easy or tough.
We always have our fun.
For we've taken toll of the whole damn lot –
The Eyetie, the Tojo and Hun.

And if at last we reach the Shangri-la,
There'll be someone to tell us, I bet,
Who'll say: 'Wait till you get to heaven or hell,
YOU AIN'T SEEN NOTHING YET.'

But before I end this story of mine,
Of the dastardly deed I must tell,
Of bastards who ratted our packs on the beach,
While we were deep in the jungle hell.

We had guarded our packs in the long years before,
From the Syrian, Gippo and Jew,
From the bedouin Arab and thieving Turk,
From the rest of the foul devil's crew.

We think we're home among our folks,
That our gear will be safe, at least,
But they pounced on our packs when we turned our backs,
Like vultures on carrion feast.

They thieved our fountain pens, tobacco – the lot,
Lined their dug-outs with our packs as well.
'Twas not enough for those pariah dogs.
May their lousy souls roast in hell.

They took out the snaps of mothers, wives and kids,
And scattered them out in the rain,
Then trampled them deep in the foul jungle mud,
A low act to cause us pain.

If this is a sample of what folks think of us,
Then it would be better by far
To have left us to fight with Montgomery's men,
Where the deeds we have done are no bar.

But I say to you – and may you never have peace –
That this truth will ever endure.
The mills of the gods grind exceedingly slow,
But they grind exceedingly sure.

For as ye sow, so shall ye reap,
On this I'll take a bet.
For when we meet, you'll know full well,
THAT YOU AIN'T SEEN NOTHING YET.

Going Round The Bend

To the tune of 'Lili Marlene'

We went out to SEAC, to finish off the war.
Before we sailed from Cochin, the blooming lot was o'er.
But we were seen by the STO,
He said, 'You cannot go.
Come round the fucking corner, come round the fucking bend.'

So right round the corner, merrily we went,
Handsomely rewarded by our fifteen per cent.
Indian fags was all to smoke –
And that's no joke.
We'd cough and choke
Around the fucking corner, around the fucking bend.

Outward bound from Hoogli, down to Singapore.
A chance of getting letters,
Be six months' old or more.
We'd all get clean,
The fleet canteen
Was round the fucking corner, round the fucking bend.

Soon we'll ship for Aussie, leaving old SEAC,
We're bloody sure that none of us are ever coming back.
Farewell Chowringhee, Kidderpore,
Your steamy shore
We'll see no more.
We're going round the corner, right round the fucking bend.

16

Demob

THE NAVY PILOTS DISCHARGE SONG
'I'll go along to Trafalgar Square
And say to old Lord Nelson . . .'

As the war dragged on and on, military song-writers' sardonic estimates as to when it would end ranged from 1950 to 1963.

The first song in this section had scores of versions, each of them fitting a different set of circumstances.

This Is My Story

To the tune of the Crusader hymn, 'Blessed Assurance'

This is my story, this is my song:
We've been in commission too fucking long.
Roll on the *Nelson*, the *Rodney*, *Renown*,
This two-funnelled bastard is getting me down.

The Gallant Ninth

This fantasy of a victory parade to be held in 1950 was written by an Australian during the seemingly interminable North African campaign.

Jack Curtin was Prime Minister of Australia, and Tom Blamey the Commander-in-Chief.

'Twas a sunny day in Sydney,
Each heart was full of joy,
And every girl who had no Yank
Was there to meet her boy.

Jack Curtin stood on the town hall steps,
Tom Blamey by his side,
Saluting each division and
Announcing them with pride.

First, here comes the gallant 6th,
Their daring deeds you know.
In Libya, they chased the Wops,
Filled Musso's heart with woe.

Greece and Crete came after that,
They gave the Huns some hell.
Originals are few today,
For most lay where they fell.

Next came the lucky 7th,
Lucky they really are.
They never saw much action,
Except in Syria.

Here come the 8th from Singapore,
We got them from the Jap,
For a ton and a half of iron ore,
And a couple of tons of scrap.

The last filed past, no more in sight,
The march it seemed was ended quite.
Then came a roar, the air it shook:
'Where are the 9th, the Rats of Tobruk?'

Jack's face turned pale,
He dropped the mike.
'I cannot tell them, Tom,' he said,
'But you can, if you like.'

Tom raised his hand. The shouting died.
He spoke in broken voice.
'It makes a damned long story, folks,
What happened to those boys.

'I had to leave them over there,
For someone had to stay,
To finish all those places,
Whose foundations I did lay.

'That was back in '42,
And now it's 1950.
I went back there the other day,
To have a quiet shufti.

'Instead of a bunch of soldiers,
I found a bunch of Wogs.
Each had a little olive grove,
A donkey, and some dogs.

'They wear those funny trousers,
That are baggy at the back.
They've forgotten their native language,
And say "Shalom" for "Jack".

'Each has a bint who does the work.
They drink wine and arrak.
The officers are doing well,
But they're baggy at the back.

'You really cannot blame them,
They have been there so long.
I thought that if I had brought them back,
I would be doing wrong.

'I hope you will not blame me,
Not blame me in the least,
For those boys seem so happy,
Back in the Middle East.'

When This War Is Over

To the tune of 'Stars of the Evening'

Oh, when this war is over we're going to get a medal,
We're going to get a medal, we're going to get a medal,
Oh, when this war is over, we're going to get a medal,
The lid of a bully beef tin.

Stars of the evening, shining on the cookhouse door,
Stars of the evening, shining on the cookhouse door.

Oh, when this war is over, we're going to get a ribbon,
We're going to get a ribbon, we're going to get a ribbon,
Oh, when this war is over, we're going to get a ribbon,
      A piece of four by two.

Stars of the evening, *etc.*

Oh, when this war is over, we're going to get a bar,
We're going to get a bar, we're going to get a bar,
Oh, when this war is over, we're going to get a bar,
      A bar of Lifebuoy soap.

Stars of the evening, *etc.*

And when this war is over, we're going to get demobbed,
We're going to get demobbed, we're going to get demobbed,
And when this war is over, we're going to get demobbed,
      In nineteen fifty-three!

Stars of the evening, *etc.*

The British Soldier's Discharge Song

When the fighting was at its fiercest
And everything looked black,
This was the promise that cheered us on:
'You'll get your old job back!'

We were not professional soldiers,
Fighting was not our game.
We were only peaceful citizens
Who fought hard just the same.

We sacrificed our wives and kids
And homes to do our bit.
But now the door is closed to us.
It seems hard, we admit.

For I can't get the old job,
And can't get a new,
Can't carry on as I used to do.
I look around me, and what do I see?

Thousands and thousands of fellows
A lot worse off than me.
In Piccadilly, friends pass me by.
I'm absolutely stranded in the Strand.

And I confess I was contented, more or less,
When I was stony broke in No Man's Land.

Repat

Even when there was no more need of them in the fighting areas, shortage of troopships afterwards meant that the servicemen had to wait on, and on, and on, for repatriation.

To the tune of 'I Can't Give You Anything But Love'

We can't get that repat down to three, fellows,
All the ships have buggered off to sea, fellows.
Fret awhile, sweat awhile, you'll soon forget,
Civvy street, slippered feet,
All the things you ever dreamed of.
We can't get that repat down to three, fellows,
Louis Mountbatten says it cannot be, fellows,
You can all box on to '63, fellows,
We can't get that repat down to three.

Jimmy

Many of the men who had married – often rather hurriedly – before going overseas had children as much as two or even three years old, whom they had never seen.

R. B. Orritt writes: 'I was serving with the Royal Marine Engineers on Somree Island, Burma, camping in the paddy fields. The Royal Marine landing craft were pulling out one particular night. Whilst waiting to move, this boy playing a small ukelele was singing this lovely little song. I need not explain how lovely and touching it was on this tropical night.'

I'm looking through the window, with Jimmy by my side,
Thinking of his daddy far away.
I'm looking through the window, with Jimmy by my side,
Wondering where and when we'll meet again.
Although there's miles and miles between us, my little laddy,
'Tween you and the one you've never seen, your daddy,
I'm looking through the window with Jimmy by my side,
Yes, thinking of his daddy far away.

The Airman's Discharge Song

Soon I will get my discharge,
And I shall say to Sarge,
You can stick the Air Force up your arse.
It's dirty, but it's done,
It's dirty, but it's fun.

The Australian Soldier's Discharge Song

To the tune of 'Home on the Range'

Oh give me a home
Where no army can roam,
Where no brass-hats or provos can stay,
Where there's no dress parades,
Or no more air raids
And no adjutants to forfeit your pay.

Oh give me a land
Which I know I can stand,
Where I won't be annoyed by those stripes.
No more waiting in queues,
While they fill me with stews,
And rice puddings that give me the gripes.

Oh for that land I pray,
Though it's far, far away,
But I'll get there someday, I'm sure.
And if I go in the army again,
I'll be barmy.
For I've had all I want of war.

And now I've found that home
Where no army can roam.
Bully beef is a thing of the past.
And though the atmosphere's hot
In this new home I've got,
I'm out of the army at last.

Back In Circulation Again

It's wonderful, so wonderful to think of the happy day,
When we can say we're back in circulation again.
We're sure to strike things lucky like a prisoner freed from the pen,
And we'll sing we're back in circulation again.
Spending our dough buying diamonds and pearls,
Swell cafés, cabarets, catching up the lost time making love to the girls,
Back to the sights, soft harbour lights,
A lot of excitement and then hear us shout,
We're back in circulation again.

The School Of War

They taught him how to use a knife,
And kill without a sound,
To swim a stream, to climb a cliff,
And burrow in the ground.

They taught him how to hate the foe,
With all-consuming rage,
Until the animal in man
Burst forth from reason's cage.

And then one day in Normandy,
His lessons served him well,
And many of the enemy
Was sent to heaven, or hell.

They pinned a medal on his breast,
And called him hero too,
And sent him back to civil life
To look for work to do.

With bounding heart he homeward sped,
Planning the things he'd say,
When he should join the one he loved,
Never to go away.

But as he entered at the door,
He stopped and stared aghast.
His wife was in another's arms!
Her love for him had passed.

The hate he'd learned in days of war
Came running through his head.
Swiftly the knife he raised on high
And struck her lover dead.

They pinned no medal on his breast.
But friendless and forlorn,
They found him guilty of his crime.
He'll hang tomorrow morn.

R. F. Palmer

The Navy Pilot's Discharge Song

Now when I am a civvy,
Dressed up in civvy clothes,
I'll go along to Trafalgar Square
And say to old Lord Nelson:
'Shove off. Get stuffed,
You fucking RN bastard.'

Index of First Lines

INDEX OF FIRST LINES